GAUDÍ AFTERNOON

Also by Barbara Wilson

Pam Nilsen Mysteries:
Murder in the Collective
Sisters of the Road
The Dog Collar Murders

Other Works:
Gaudí Afternoon
Cows and Horses
Miss Venezuela

GAUDÍ AFTERNOON
BARBARA WILSON

The Seal Press

Acknowledgements

I would like to thank the Seattle Arts Commission Individual Artists Program, whose support helped with the development of this work, and the following individuals for reading and commenting on the manuscript in various stages: Rebecca Brown, Faith Conlon, Dorsey Green, Richard Labonté, Ruthie Petrie, Rachel Pollack and Linda Semple. A special thanks to Candace Coughlin of Barcelona.

Cover art by Jana Rekosh
Cover design by Clare Conrad

Library of Congress Cataloging-in-Publication Data

Wilson, Barbara, 1950-
    Gaudí afternoon / Barbara Wilson.
        p.   cm.
    ISBN 0-931188-89-X : $8.95
    I. Title.
    PS3573.I45678G38   1990
    813'.54--dc20   90-8675
                                                                   CIP

Printed in the United States of America
First printing, October 1990
10 9 8 7 6 5 4 3 2 1

Foreign Distribution:
In Canada: Raincoast Book Distribution, Vancouver, B.C.
In Great Britain and Europe: Airlift Book Company, London.
In Australia: Stilone, N.S.W.

For Becky

For Gaudí, however, nature consisted of forces
that work beneath the surface,
which was merely
an expression
of those
inner
forces.

Rainier Zerbst, *Antoni Gaudí*

1

My name is Cassandra Reilly and I don't live anywhere. At least that's what I tell people when they ask. I was raised in Kalamazoo, Michigan, but I left when I was sixteen and I can hardly remember when that was. I have an Irish passport and make a sort of living as a translator, chiefly of Spanish, and chiefly of South American novels, at least at the moment. I rent an upstairs room in a tall Georgian house in Hampstead and another room in Oakland, California from an old friend Lucy Hernandez. These are my most permanent residences, by which I mean I receive mail there. But often as not I'm travelling: a conference here, a book fair there, a yen to see some part of the world I don't know yet. On my way back from Hong Kong I'll get an urge to see a friend in Kyoto and end up teaching English in Japan for two months. Or I'll decide I need to catch up with an old lover in Uruguay, and political events will keep me there longer than I expected.

I'm rarely anywhere more than a few months at a time and that's the way I like it. Of course my Irish relatives in County Cork believe my real spiritual home is Ballybarnacle, and sometimes I believe it too. Ireland is always green and magical in my mind and sometimes—on a crowded train snaking through India, on a sweltering day in a Columbian jail—I long for its mists and rocky shores. But hardly ever when I'm there.

I had been back in London for almost three months after a challenging six weeks in Iceland visiting a new friend, the volcano expert Ingrid Biritsdotter. Money was tight and I had been

3

forced to take on a larger translation project than I generally like—a lavishly written, complicated novel by the fourteenth writer to be compared to García Márquez. Actually, it was by a woman, so she was only the fifth author to be dubbed "the new female García Márquez."

Gloria de los Angeles was her pen name, and her wildly popular novel was entitled *La Grande y su hija*—literally, *The Big One and Her Daughter*. Told by a young woman, María, it had jungles and decaying colonial cities, plagues and miracles, a sinister villain called Raoul, a revolutionary named Eduardo and strong women like Cristobel, María's mother and the *Grande* of the title, who nevertheless was reduced to quivering guava jelly whenever Eduardo emerged from the jungle. Gloria de los Angeles was a Venezuelan mother of four, I had learned, who had previously translated Jackie Collins and Danielle Steel into Spanish. *La Grande y su hija* had swept Spain and South America and was poised, so the British publisher believed, to do the same in England and North America. A better title would help, though the English editor hadn't liked the American agent's suggestion: *Big Mama's Baby Daughter*.

I was up to page two hundred and forty-five and still had about seventy-five pages of the first draft to go. My deadline was June 1, two months away. I had saved time by not reading the book in advance, which had the added advantage of keeping me in a continual state of astonishment at Gloria de los Angeles's inventive plot line.

In any other country it would have been spring, but England keeps its own counsel about the weather, and had decided that a few more weeks of sleet, hail and freezing winds were good for the English, the one people on earth who think you should feel damp and chilled inside as well as outside. Up in my room it was cozy; a few days ago, in honor of it being the first of April, I had turned off one of my heaters, but tonight I had it back on again. I was surrounded at my desk, in fact, by four heaters. When you get into your forties it's harder to keep warm on your own anymore.

From downstairs I could hear the faint sounds of a Vivaldi

bassoon concerto. Olivia Wulf, who owned the house, was a former first violinist with the English Chamber Orchestra. Now in her seventies, she was wheelchair-bound and cared for by her old friend and mine Nicola Gibbons, an accomplished bassoonist and Vivaldi scholar. In the evening the two of them often liked to arrange small baroque concerts for themselves. Although months and occasionally years went by between my stays here, this house, even more than the one in Oakland, was my post office, clothes closet and information center. I might forget in the deepest Amazon what new cultural and political developments were really significant, but when I came back to London I could count on Nicky, an ardent socialist-feminist as well as a fervent theater- and concert-goer, to help me get caught up.

I had just plunged into Chapter Twelve, which opened:

When I was thirteen a series of flash fires mysteriously combusted all through the river basin, causing no great harm to villages or to the jungle dwellers, animal or human, but great alarm to the parrots which scattered like leaves before a storm, blood-red and shrieking dementedly. I was not to know this for years but the fires coincided with the menopause of my long-lost mother Cristobel, who, lying in a darkened room of her great shabby palace in the city, her ivory forehead covered in cool cloths smelling faintly of rosewater, and remembering the scenes of her youth, was lighting conflagrations of memory along the banks of the fabulous river of silver,

when the phone rang and, shortly after, a gong sounded far below to let me know that I should pick up the line.

The voice on the phone was American; there was a weak buzzing in the background that made it clear the call was coming from across the Atlantic. Across a few dozen states as well.

"Is this Cassandra Reilly?"

"Speaking."

It was a woman with a pleasantly husky voice, slightly distorted by the long-distance crackling. "You don't know me but

I'm a friend of Lucy's in Oakland. My name is Frankie Stevens."

"Yes?" I was hesitant. Lucy might be one of my oldest friends, but I had just gotten rid of one visitor, someone's Alaskan cousin visiting Europe for the first time, and wasn't eager to play hostess again for a year or two.

The contralto voice paused. "I've got a slight problem and Lucy thought you might be able to help me. Since you speak Spanish."

"A translation job?" Again, I wasn't overly enthusiastic. The last friend of a friend who'd called up had wanted me to translate a computer program on managing your own vineyard from Spanish to English. Besides, I was up to my armpits with innocent but wise Cristobel and her diabolical first husband Raoul.

"Well, yes. Look—I wonder if we might talk about this in person? I'm flying to Heathrow this evening and that will put me in London tomorrow afternoon. I'll be staying at a hotel near Russell Square. Can we meet?"

I hesitated loudly.

Frankie said, "I'll make it worth your while."

I doubted that. Still, what was the harm? Even if Frankie were to propose the preposterous it couldn't be more bizarre than anything in this novel. And I probably needed a break—I was starting to lose my grip on reality.

So I suggested we meet in the Abyssinian rooms at the British Museum. Four p.m. Frankie said she would be wearing red.

The Abyssinians were not people with whom you'd probably enjoy spending a spring day, rainy or sunny. They seemed like the kind of guys who would enslave you as soon as look at you. The friezes were full of long lines of captives in chains, carrying animal, vegetable and mineral tribute and looking glum and apprehensive, no doubt for good reason. I was very fond, however, of the wavy river lines at the bottom of the friezes and the fish that jumped through them.

I was right on time but there was no woman in red in sight. I hadn't known how to describe myself. My last lover called me "dessicated," but that, I'm sure, was just pique that I had called things off first. On the other hand, age *has* made me a bit scrawny and tough, and it's hard to pamper one's skin on the road. On my better days I believe I resemble the middle-aged Katherine Hepburn.

Today I was dressed in a warm wool jumpsuit and my black leather bomber jacket. My hair, which one hairstylist had referred to as an Irish Afro, was bundled up under a black beret with an old *Troops Out Now* button. I wear my beret and my political sentiments whenever I meet prospective clients whom I suspect might be thinking of taking advantage of me.

I waited and waited. I hoped that Frankie hadn't been stopped at immigration. Maybe she was a drug dealer and I'd be implicated through a traced phone call. The narcotics squad would break into my attic room, take one look at my South American newspaper clippings and peg me for a coca baroness.

The Abyssinian rooms were not crowded, even on this rainy day when tourists flooded the museum. Most of the visitors were huddled around the Egyptian mummies and the Elgin Marbles. Only a few Japanese tourists, multiply-cameraed, peered with me at the long rows of captives and warriors. I fell into a kind of reverie about history, war and violence, and was only roused by the jaunty energy of someone advancing towards me.

A woman in a stretchy bright red tunic, black mini-skirt and black tights came tripping lightly as a gymnast over the stone floor. Her lipstick was a cheerful gash against her pale face and she wore a dozen red and black plastic bangles around her thin white wrists. Something about her face appealed to me right away; it was impish with a triangular chin and widely-spaced hazel eyes. Her hair was auburn and chaotically, delightfully curly, corkscrewed like that of a Shirley Temple doll. She was in her late twenties.

She skidded to a stop in front of me; on her feet were silly pointed black shoes. She wrinkled her nose. "Cassandra?"

"Frankie?"

You could tell she was American: the first thing she did was throw her arms around me and squeeze me tight. "Glad to meet you!"

Frankie reminded me of a young Irish setter, leggy, friendly, frisky. Upstairs, where I took her for tea, she beamed at the waitresses behind the counter and told the woman at the cash register to have a nice day.

"This is my first time in London," she said dramatically. "And you know what my first thought was? Wow, they really do talk like *Masterpiece Theater*. You're lucky to live here." She polished off a scone with strawberry jam and lit a Camel. "And I just can't thank you enough for agreeing to help me."

"I haven't agreed to anything," I reminded her pleasantly.

"Oh, I know," she said quickly and wrinkled her nose, as if we were already complicit. "Agreeing to meet me, I mean... Lucy spoke so highly of you... I felt sure you'd be the right person for this job, and now that I've met you I'm positive."

She looked at me brightly, and repeated, "You just seem *right.*"

"What exactly is this job?" I asked.

"It's simple, really," she said. "I'm looking for someone in Barcelona and I need a translator to go with me."

"Barcelona!" I said. I loved Barcelona. "I'm in the middle of a big project here," I said. "I can't just take off and go to Barcelona."

"Oh, it wouldn't be for long," she assured me. "A few days maybe. Not more than a week. I'll pay your round-trip airfare of course, and a hundred dollars a day for expenses. Whether or not you're able to find the person I'm looking for I'll pay you a thousand dollars, but if you do find him, it will be three thousand. Think about it, Cassandra," she said, in a deeper drawl, "three thousand for just a few days work."

I *was* thinking. Thinking about the dim shabby streets and pouring rain outside, thinking about Cristobel and Raoul waiting for me in my little upstairs room, thinking about the thin blue letter I'd received a week ago from my friend Ana in Barcelona.

"Who's 'him'?" I asked. "And why me?"

"My husband, Ben." Frankie sighed significantly, tossed her auburn corkscrews and lit another Camel with her silver lighter. "It's *so* complicated. You see, we've been separated for about five years, but we're still close. We married in college. I didn't know then he was gay and I didn't know he was from a wealthy family. Ben persuaded me to move to San Francisco and that's where he came out. He didn't want his family to know, so we agreed to stay married. At first it was hard on me, but eventually I accepted it. I'm an actress, you see, and both my freedom and Ben's economic support are important to me."

"You're an actress?" I said. I'd always had a weakness for girls behind the footlights.

"A stage actress," she smiled. "Unlike most of my friends, when I'm between roles I don't have to waitress. I'm *so* spoiled really!" She wrinkled her nose again, and rounded her bright hazel eyes. I could imagine her playing the gamine on stage, the saucy soubrette with the husky voice.

"What's the problem then?"

Frankie frowned. "The *problem* is that Ben is such a free spirit. He's never had to work and sometimes he just takes off for a month or two without telling me. Which is usually fine, but this time I happened to get a call from the family lawyer saying Ben needed to sign some important papers. I stalled as much as I could while I tried to find Ben, but after a few days I realized he'd simply disappeared."

Frankie paused and leaned over the table conspiratorially. "The papers are terribly important of course, but it's far worse if his father gets wind of the fact that I, his *wife*, don't live with him anymore and that I have absolutely no idea where to find him. His family is very traditional. They might cut him out of the will or something."

"What makes you think he's in Barcelona?"

"I started going through his phone bills," Frankie said without embarrassment. "I have a key to his apartment of course, so

I just went through his desk, found the phone bills and started calling some of the numbers. There were quite a few to a number in Spain, in Barcelona. Whoever it was who answered only spoke Spanish, but when I said, 'Ben? Is Ben there?' they panicked and said in English, 'There's no Ben here,' and hung up the phone. So you can see why I think that's the logical place to start."

"And money's no object?" I asked.

"And time is of the essence." She smiled and placed her bangled hand on mine. "I hope you'll help me. You see, I ran into your friend Lucy Hernandez—who I knew years ago—as I was leaving Ben's apartment in the Castro. I told her that I was thinking of going to Barcelona but that I didn't know any Spanish and it would be a real problem for me. So she suggested you since you're a translator. I flew to London to persuade you. I plan to leave in a few hours. I'm hoping you'll follow me as soon as you can."

I was more than persuaded, but some last remaining shred of caution made me hesitate. "The thousand is up front, then, no strings attached?"

Frankie took out a red leather purse from inside an enormous glossy black shoulder bag. She pulled out an envelope and put it on the table in front of me. I'm sure the rest of the tea room thought we were doing a drug transaction or an IRA arms deal.

"Your airline ticket on Iberia is inside, and ten hundred dollar bills."

"What made you so sure of me?" I asked, taking the envelope.

Frankie gave the charming smile of a woman who has always gotten what she wanted. "Feminine intuition?"

2

There is a winding street in the Barri Gòtic or Gothic Quarter of Barcelona, not far from the cathedral, where you can pass one antique and curio shop after another. Whenever I find myself in Barcelona I invariably end up on Carrer Banys Nous, drifting by plate-glass windows through which you can see heavy wooden chests, rococo paintings in gold leaf frames and opulent tea sets and ceramics. Because I travel so much I rarely buy anything—but I still like to look.

But on one occasion, seven or eight years ago, I found myself with an impossible, irresistible desire to buy a ship's figurehead in one of the small shops. Long in the torso, with bright gilded hair and slightly parted roseate lips, the figurehead leaned forward through enormous pink- and purple-striped conches and blushing open scallops in the display window as if she could feel the Caribbean air still fresh on her painted cheeks.

Never before had I gone into any of the shops, not even to inquire a price. I'd been content to window shop, not to possess. But that day, almost without thinking, inflamed by desire, I rushed into the dark shop interior.

It was a tiny place, packed neat as a ship's cabin. On the walls were paintings of ships at sea and worn old maps; from the ceiling hung lanterns and finely detailed model ships. At the back of the shop the owner and a customer were just beginning to negotiate a purchase—of the ship's figurehead in the window.

I begged, I pleaded, I said that I thought my family had owned the figurehead, that I had been a sailor in a former life, that I would die if I couldn't have this lovely carved wooden lady. I offered to pay anything the owner wanted. He tried to play us off against each other, obviously seeing a profit whichever way he turned. But the other customer was adamant—and disarming. With great logic and single-mindedness she talked me out of my desire. Then invited me for dinner in one of Barcelona's best restaurants. We'd been friends ever since.

Now I sat in Ana's enormous apartment at midnight, drinking tea with her in the kitchen. It hadn't taken me long to rush home from the British Museum, throw a few things into a bag and scribble a hasty note to Nicky. At the last minute I grabbed *La Grande y su hija* and threw that in too.

Ana, tall and slender, was wearing her usual: jeans and a white long-sleeved shirt rolled up over her thin wrists, cowboy boots that she had probably picked up in Italy. Her dark chestnut hair was pulled away from her oval face in a heavy braid down her back. She always looked beautiful, and never any different.

"When I wrote you two weeks ago I never dreamed you'd respond so quickly," she was saying.

I tried to think what her letter had said. Lots about her work, something about being lonely. . . . I put on a sympathetic look. "It's been hard for you since Lydia went back to Argentina, hasn't it?"

"Lydia was a mad woman," Ana shrugged. "It's not Lydia so much. But this apartment can sometimes seem very big. It needs more life in it. Cassandra," she fixed me with her soft brown eyes, "I'm so glad you're here."

"So am I," I said warily. This didn't sound at all like my independent friend Ana, who mocked Relationships almost as often as I did. "Of course I'll be busy a lot, but I still hope we can get together for good long chats."

She winced slightly at the word chats. I hoped she didn't really think. . . no. . . she knew my character, she couldn't possibly. . . .

I changed the subject. "Why don't you show me what you've been working on?"

When you asked her, Ana said she had always wanted to be an architect, she didn't know why. But her ideas for buildings had proved so flighty and improbable that no architectural firm would hire her after university, and she had been reduced to creating fantastic houses for the small children of the wealthy. These houses were shaped exactly to the child's fantasies. After consultation with a child who said, "I want a house like a cat," for example, Ana would create a house curved like a sleeping Siamese from stuffed almond and brown velvet. If a girl fantasized about trains, Ana would build her a cardboard locomotive and sleeper, with a rear car for her baby sister; if a boy imagined a jungle, Ana's house for him would be painted with lianas and tiled with orchids and monkeys.

All the rooms and closets of this enormous apartment were filled with construction materials and curios that Ana had picked up from dumpsters as well as antique shops. The living room, because of its huge dimensions, was her workroom, and at the moment it contained three projects in various stages.

The first house under construction was built on a wooden frame, a stuffed chambered nautilus five feet high with large and small compartments and a spiralling corridor. It had appliquéd designs of fish and shells all over its striped fabric exterior.

The second was a giant jewelry box made of wood and covered in blue plush. It had two drawers, the top one for sleeping in and the bottom for playing in. It even had a lifesize ballerina on top, made of padded cotton with a stiff net skirt and a blue velvet bodice. If you pushed a button, she spun around to the strains of the Blue Danube waltz.

"I'm still working on the speed," Ana said absent-mindedly. "If you make it too fast her skirt will rip off the child's face; but if she goes too slow she looks crippled."

The third project was in unassembled pieces of gaudy papier-maché all over the floor. I saw what looked like a painted woman's thigh and a colorful single breast.

"This is a house for a woman giving birth," Ana said, picking up the thigh as if that would explain something.

We curled up on some pillows and I told her about Frankie, trying not to make it sound as if that were the only reason I'd come.

Ana said, "I don't know, it sounds like a wild goose chase. Barcelona is enormous. And even if you find this husband of hers, is it as simple as Frankie is making it out to be? What if she's out for revenge for some reason and plans to kill him?"

"Frankie seems absolutely harmless. A little dramatic, but after all, she's an actress. Her real story may be different than the one she's telling me, but I hardly think she's a murderer."

"It's you I'm worried about," Ana said with an embarrassment she tried to mask as severity. "Remember the last time you were here. That business with Carmen."

"Carmen," I mused, remembering. "I'll definitely have to get in touch with Carmen."

"I hope you'll have time for *me*."

"I always have time for you, Ana," I said. "What's wrong, anyway?"

She looked at me wistfully. "I want my life to change, that's all."

Oh god, next she'd be talking about babies.

"I want a child."

"I think we should sleep on this, Ana. Let's talk about it tomorrow, okay?"

She sighed and got up.

"Just don't plan on spending all your time with Carmen," she warned.

"Ana, really. I'm here to work."

But before I went to sleep I looked at the ship's figurehead that Ana had thoughtfully placed in my guest bedroom, and I remembered the single-minded expression of Ana's that day in the antique shop. She had something on her mind that had to do with me.

Babies.

✦

Frankie and I had agreed to meet the next morning at ten. I woke early and went down to the Café Zurich across from the Plaça de Catalunya. Even though it was only seven-thirty the streets were lively. Spaniards get up early and go to bed late, and I do the same when I'm in Spain. It must be all that coffee. But it also has a lot to do with the heat. Barcelona on this morning was cool and fresh, the sidewalks newly washed, only a light buzz of car exhaust in the air. I sat down at a table at the Café Zurich and thanked god I was here. Unlike London, where the most you could hope for in the morning on your way to work was a slop of milk in a weak brown stew, snatched in some horrid tea shop with linoleum tables and greasy windows, in Barcelona you could sit outside at your own table and the waiter would appear before you with a cup and two pitchers on his tray. From one pitcher he would pour a shot of black coffee, from the other a stream of hot milk. With a flourish: "*Señora.*"

And it was spring in Barcelona too, real spring, not drizzly on-and-off spring. England could have its lilacs under gray skies; I was relieved to be here where I could see plane trees overhanging the Ramblas and women going to work dressed like movie stars. I'd exchanged my leather bomber jacket for a printed Japanese wraparound shirt, and on my head I'd wound a purple and black turban.

I read *El País* and *La Vanguardia,* watched the bustle around me, had another coffee and two croissants and finally set off down the Ramblas, the long street that is Barcelona's heart. It's really made up of five separate streets, but they all flow into each other. The central tree-lined walkway is almost always crowded and the kiosks sell rabbits, canaries and roses as well as postcards and newspapers from all over the world.

I walked midway down to the Plaça Boquería and turned into a side street to reach the three small squares around the church of Santa María del Pi. I had suggested a small hotel off the Plaça del Pi to Frankie and was meeting her at a café outside a nearby bar.

15

She was waiting for me, more fragile than when we'd parted at the steps of the British Museum, less jaunty and more querulous. My heart sank a little as I approached her table and she turned accusing eyes on me.

"They put me in a room by the elevator shaft, I couldn't sleep a wink all night for the noise, and the bed was too soft. The man at the desk doesn't speak a word of English so I couldn't complain to him. I'm feeling absolutely ragged."

It was true, she didn't look her best, even though she had made an effort. She had on her bangles and her red red lipstick and her silly little pointed shoes. But in the bright morning sun her pale skin looked sallow and slightly scarred with acne. Her ashtray was already full and she coughed between her words.

I produced soothing noises and promised to find her another hotel if she wanted. Frankie, stage trooper that she was, struggled to cheer up. "Americans abroad, we're pathetic, aren't we?"

And I liked her again.

We ordered more coffee and I decided to have another croissant. The tables outside the Bar del Pi were full this morning: three Germans telling each other travelling stories, a couple of young women in black with art portfolios at their feet, a mother and her grown pregnant daughter, both looking quite pleased with themselves, and a lone scientist with a flight bag on the seat next to him. The flight bag was imprinted with the words EUROPEAN SOCIETY FOR ORGAN TRANSPLANTATION.

Frankie took out a scrap of paper from her huge purse. "Well, we might as well get started," she said briskly. "Here's the phone number I called. What you need to do is get the address and give it to me."

"How do you suggest I do that?"

"That's up to you." Her tone was curt, then she remembered the charm. "I have so much confidence in you, Cassandra. Don't mind me, it's probably jet lag."

I took the piece of paper and went into the bar to use the phone. I would use the only ruse I could think of—I'd pretend I had a wrong number.

"Hello." A man's voice answered the phone. He was speaking Catalan with what sounded like an American accent.

I asked, in Castilian, to speak to Isabella.

No Isabella lived here, he answered, switching to Castilian.

That was impossible. This was 99–67–73 and Isabella must be there.

She wasn't, he repeated, and made as if to hang up.

I got worked up. That was completely impossible! Isabella had given me this number herself! Was he saying that Isabella would make a mistake about her own number? Then he didn't know Isabella!

He admitted with some irritation that he didn't know Isabella.

This was 99–67–73, I accused. Isabella lived there, right on València, number 34. I had been there, I knew.

This wasn't València, he said triumphantly. It was Provença.

It wasn't València? I allowed a small hint of doubt to creep into my voice. Not number 34?

"Provença, 261," he repeated, and put down the phone.

I returned to the table. "It's on Provença Street, number 261."

Frankie looked shocked. "They told you, just like that?"

"No, of course not. I used subterfuge." With real pleasure I surveyed the little square, the sooty church, the leisurely bustle of mid-morning. "You want to go there right now?"

Frankie lit another cigarette and finished her coffee. "Could you order me another one?"

"The man I talked to had an American accent," I said. "But he spoke both Catalan and Castilian."

"Ben only speaks Spanish," Frankie said.

"Castilian *is* Spanish. Catalan is what they speak in Barcelona."

"They don't speak Spanish here? Someone should have told me. No wonder they didn't understand me at the hotel desk when I tried to use my phrasebook."

"They do speak Spanish as well," I explained patiently. "But Catalan is their language and many people refuse to speak

Castilian on principle. It goes back to the years when Franco tried to eradicate the Catalan language and culture. The first time I came to Barcelona, over twenty years ago, all the signs were in Castilian, and you could be fined for speaking Catalan on the streets."

Frankie was uninterested. "Well I'm sure Ben doesn't know Catalan."

"Do you have any idea who it might have been? Has Ben ever mentioned a friend in Barcelona?"

"If he had I wouldn't have had to employ you, would I?" snapped Frankie, then she murmured apologetically. "Sorry, I'm not myself this morning. I just don't want to be rushed, that's all. I mean, at least now we know the address, that's the important thing."

I restrained myself. Obviously I was in a rush, but whether it was in order to collect my two thousand dollars or to overcome the doubts that were beginning to form, was hard to say.

Frankie smoked and drank another cup of coffee. The lovely spring sun beat down upon us and the German tourists departed to be replaced by a woman with a baby in a stroller.

"Look," she said finally, "It's a little more complicated than I let on yesterday in London."

Somehow I wasn't that surprised.

"It's not that Ben and I aren't good *friends,*" she said. "But— in actual fact—we're divorced. Everything else is true," she hastened to assure me. "About his being gay and his family not knowing and us needing to keep it a secret—"

"If you're such good friends," I broke in, "why would he be upset to get a visit from you in Barcelona? Especially if you're trying to give him something to sign for his family."

Frankie sighed. "Ben is such an independent person, it's hard to explain. He's independent and. . . irresponsible. He just gets it into his head to do things. . . sometimes against his best interests. . . . "

"The paper is something he might not want to sign?"

"Oh no," Frankie dismissed that idea with a rattle of bangles.

18

"Not if he's approached in the right way," she amended. "He hates to feel pressured."

"And he might feel pressured if he thought you had flown halfway around the world to get him to sign it."

"That's not it at all," Frankie pouted. "And there's no point in you being so antagonistic. *After all,* it's not like we know it's even Ben you talked to. I just want to know what kind of situation I'm walking into. Isn't that reasonable?"

"Yesss," I said. "So how do you want to go about this then?"

"I want you to go over to the place he lives and just watch and see who comes in and out the door."

"Dozens of people probably live in his building," I protested. "Do you have a photograph of him?"

Once again Frankie seemed inappropriately taken aback. "Oh, ah, no. I should have thought of that."

"Well, is he tall or short, what color is his hair, what kind of clothes does he wear?"

"He's ... medium-height ... regular-looking ... short hair ... He wears, I don't know, normal clothes. Jeans." Frankie was floundering and I had no idea why.

"So I'm supposed to stand outside this building and look for a regular guy with absolutely no identifying marks?" I rebelled. "I think it's pointless, I really do. How am I going to describe him to you?"

"We'll get you a camera," she said. "You can take photographs of everyone who goes in and comes out."

"That should make me really inconspicuous."

"A small hidden camera," Frankie said, taking out a gold American Express card.

That cheered me up somewhat. If she had a gold card she wasn't hurting for money. But I added one condition:

"I get to keep the camera."

3

Barcelona is a divided city. Below the Plaça de Catalunya, a vast square enlivened by fountains and marred by stretches of artificial grass, the streets are ancient and narrow, gradually twisting their way from the modish leather and shoe shops, gorgeous patisseries and restaurants of the Barri Gòtic down to the tenements by the port, to the Chinese Quarter or Barri Xines— a warren of seedy hotels and squalid *hostales,* with bars on every corner and long strands of laundry draped back and forth across streets where sunlight never comes. There are social divisions all the way down the Ramblas to the statue of Christopher Columbus on the sea front—the streets above the Plaça Reial are richer than below, the left side of the Ramblas is much safer than the right—but they are differences of degree, not of scale.

Above the Plaça de Catalunya Barcelona is almost another city, built on a nineteenth-century plan, not a Gothic one. In the Middle Ages grandeur meant the cathedral and later the gloomy palaces along Carrer de Montcada; in the nineteenth century the wealthy industrialists and bankers wanted enormous boulevards for their carriages, and opulent banks and shops where the ceilings were twenty feet high. Thus the Passeig de Gràcia is less like a street than an enormous thoroughfare into the architectural imagination of the previous century. Even the sidewalks are wider than most streets in the old quarter, and tiled with slate blue stones covered with swirling shell and flower patterns.

The address the man had given me, 261 Provença, was in the

nineteenth-century part of Barcelona, not far from the apartment that Ana had inherited from her wealthy grandmother. I walked unhurriedly up Gràcia, past bank after bank, shop after shop. There was one of Antoni Gaudí's buildings, the Casa Batlló, with its shimmering greeny mosaic facade and rippling rooftop, all curves and waves. Its roof has been called the "reptile's back" for its vertebrae of ceramic pots, joined to make a closed gutter. As I passed it in admiration I realized I wasn't far from La Pedrera, another famous Gaudí construction on Gràcia. It was on the corner of Provença. Some guidebooks call it Casa Milà, but its official nickname is La Pedrera, the Stone Quarry.

Provença. 261 Provença. Ben was living in La Pedrera.

I sank onto a white-tiled, curved bench across the street and considered how to approach the task Frankie had given me.

It's a massive thing, this gray-white, five-story apartment building that dominates the corner with its porous stone facing, thick columns, cave-like windows, and serpentine balconies decorated with thickets of wrought-iron vegetation. Undulating like the reflection of a stone sculpture in water, La Pedrera has a three-dimensional feel that goes beyond architecture; it doesn't give the sense of having been constructed from building materials according to blueprints, but of having risen up from the depths of the ocean.

It would be impossible to photograph everyone going in the main door on Gràcia. There were six tours a day and a constant stream of tourists with cameras walking back and forth. I got up and went inside a music shop to see if I could spy on the Provença doorway from behind a stack of cassettes, but the windows facing the street were covered with posters. I bought a half-price cassette of Gregorian Chants from Medieval Transylvania and went back outside and crossed the street.

Both entrances were wide open so that ostensibly anyone could enter. But in order to actually get upstairs you would have to use an elevator located directly behind the *portero*'s desk.

Inside the main entrance I had a chat with the *portero*, who told me that La Pedrera had recently been bought by a bank that was working on restoring it and eventually opening up at least one of the apartments for viewing. At the moment the tour only went to the roof. Who lives in the building now? I asked. One of the original owners, an old lady who bought in when Gaudí was still alive, he told me proudly. And other tenants who've been here a long time, decades. And there are the businesses of course. Any Americans living here? I asked. Oh no. He sounded shocked.

I said I'd come back for the tour a little later and went out again and sat down at an aluminum table outside a bar called La Pedrera. From here I had a clear view of the doorway. I ordered a mineral water and a *bocadillo de tortilla*, and took out my copy of *La Grande y su hija* and my notebook. The camera was on a strap inside my Japanese shirt and every time I saw a likely suspect I snapped his picture.

There weren't too many likely suspects and I didn't know if that was good or bad. The tourists were obvious of course, their cameras a dead giveaway. They walked slowly, with their necks craned up at the enormous glass doors, leaded into amoeba-like shapes that seemed to bubble up from small to large. There was what appeared to be a private school on the first floor, and teenagers came and left at regular intervals. There were workmen in blue, the inevitable cigarettes dangling, and a stone-faced woman who was vigorously sweeping the sidewalk in front of the door.

I had another mineral water and some Sevillana olives and translated from Chapter Twelve:

As the years progressed Cristobel took on the name *La Grande* because of her enormous size. In her youth my mother had been considered almost too frail and small to survive and it was only by eating far past her capacities that Cristobel had managed to hang on to survival so that, in the years to come, whenever Cristobel felt the least panic about death, her own or those near to her like Raoul first and then Eduardo, she would begin to eat as if possessed: ordering enormous meals of corn and potatoes dripping with butter, whole pigs wrapped in leaves, thick fruit drinks and entire bakeries of bread and pies. I, who was never to outgrow my childhood appellation, the Miniature, was revolted and strangely moved by stories of my mother's gross appetite.

I began to get hungry myself and rather bored. I found myself wondering if the man on the phone had said the first address that came into his head. If so, I was in for a tedious afternoon.

Still, it was Frankie's money, and if she wanted to waste my hundred-dollar-a-day fee stationing me outside La Pedrera, it was up to her. It wasn't as if I hadn't had many slow afternoons in my life: waiting for a ride in Afghanistan with two teaspoons of water in my canteen; waiting at the Romanian border while the police went through every single article I owned; waiting in a dusty jail in Tucson when I was sixteen for my mother to show up and claim me as a runaway.

I took photos for two hours and then I ran out of film. I saw mothers with children, well-dressed Spanish secretaries and bosses, workmen in blue and lots of students. I saw couples and families but mostly individuals just going about their business. Almost everyone who went in came out again, until around two when the businesses closed for the *siesta* and some of the residents of La Pedrera came home for lunch.

I didn't see a "regular" American-looking man in jeans, though I saw plenty of teenagers in pre-washed Levis and more than a few tee-shirts and sweatshirts with words in English.

Finally, about three, when traffic in and out of the building seemed to slow to almost nothing, I decided I could risk a short break. I paid my bill and put away María the Miniature and her mother and then I dashed up Gràcia a few blocks, across the Avinguda Diagonal, to a quiet street off the Carrer Major. Carmen tended to work through the closing hours of the *siesta* because that was the only time many women could come to her hairdressing salon. If I were lucky she would not only cut my hair but offer me some refreshments and some gossip.

She was shampooing an older woman when I came in, but

rushed over nevertheless and, with wet, sudsy hands, embraced me.

"Cassandra, you're so inconvenient," she said happily. "And that turban tells me you're long overdue for my scissors. Sit down, right away. My hands itch when I look at you."

She'd said that the first time we'd met a year or so before, and I'd taken her at her word. We'd had two weeks together that neither of us would ever forget, but that neither was tempted to think was any more than a fling. Carmen's main mission in life was, after all, to cut hair. She had her mother to think about. And the pope.

She handed over her shampooed customer to an assistant and ran her long manicured fingers through my gray-brown frizz which, liberated from its turban, flowed out like a cloud of fog over my shoulders. "I think I'm changing my mind about gray," she announced. "When it's under control [she emphasized *control* with a vicious snip of her scissors], it can be very elegant."

"You know best, *querida*," I said. "But I don't have much time. I'm staking out a building."

She sent an apprentice out for coffee and attacked my head with relish, talking non-stop. Under her hands my hair took on different fantastic shapes, like Gaudí buildings under construction. I watched her in the mirror: big-hipped and big-breasted, in high heels and stretch pants with a leopardskin print top, Carmen wore more make-up than Frankie or than any of my London friends would believe could look good on a face. Brown and gold eyeshadow matched her frosted bronze hair; her lips were a luscious peachy gold and her fingernails, long perfect ovals, were the same shade. She had a gold tooth she was proud of and a vaultsworth of gold jewelry. Her perfume was Opium and it was heavy.

Carmen was from Granada and never let anyone forget it. She would never want to go back there to live, she confided once, it was too backward, too Catholic, too anti-woman. But that didn't mean it hadn't far more history and culture than Barcelona. "*Los moros, La Alhambra, todo eso,*" Carmen would say, dismissing the Catalan heritage. "Our history in Granada is very old."

She refused to learn more than a few words of Catalan, and considered women like Ana, from old Catalan families, snobbish and too Europeanized. Carmen was suspicious of Europe. She made an exception for expatriate Americans like me and a few English people. She had once travelled to London and remained very impressed by the red buses and the men in the City who still wore bowler hats.

"There!" she finally said, spinning me around on the chair. I wasn't sure I liked it: long on top and closely cut on the sides and back. My neck felt cold.

But I smiled and got up to go, and only then did Carmen remember what I'd said earlier.

"What do you mean, staking out a building?"

"La Pedrera," I said. "I've taken up architecture."

"This is some crazy thing you're involved in, I feel it. How long are you going to be in Barcelona? Are you in trouble? Tell me."

I gave her a kiss on the cheek as I got up. "I'll be in Barcelona long enough to see you again. What about meeting me tonight, later?"

I winked and she drew herself up on her heels.

"I'll think about it," she said loftily.

I knew she would too, all afternoon.

Back at La Pedrera I joined the four o'clock tour, just for something different. With all the other tourists I milled about in the dim stone foyer, reading about Antoni Gaudí on the display boards.

Antoni Gaudí (1852–1926) is considered the most outstanding Catalan architect of Modernism, the art movement that flourished in Europe during the first years of this century and whose typical traits are a variety of forms and a wealth of ornamentation.

Gaudí was born in Reus, in a family of artisans where he learned the traditional crafts that he was later to use in his works. In 1878 he received his degree in architecture and from 1880 to 1926 he worked, above all in Barcelona.

His most important works in this city are the Parc Güell, the garden-city built between 1900 and 1914 in the north of the city; Casa Batlló (1904–1906) on Passeig de Gràcia; the cathedral Sagrada Família (begun in 1883 and still uncompleted) and La Pedrera or Casa Milà (1906–1912), one of the most innovative creations in international architecture.

And of course the display mentioned the manner of Gaudí's death. He had been run down by a streetcar and, unrecognized, taken to the poor hospital where he died.

The display had this to say about La Pedrera:

The conception of the inner areas and patios, the two entrances, the underground carriage park, the majestic facade, the undulating mansard and the original terrace dotted with ceramic-coated chimneys and ventilating flues endow La Pedrera with a striking personality which some have linked with European expressionism and others have defined as an anticipation of surrealism.

After a brief introduction our guide directed us to the back of the foyer and up many flights of stairs. Huffing and puffing we arrived in the attic just below the roof, which had been remodeled to provide small studios and apartments. Then we emerged onto the roof, to the sky and to a wonderful view of Barcelona from the mountains to the sea. In the near distance you could see the many spires of the unfinished cathedral Sagrada Família.

The rooftop's extraordinary aspect lay in the chimneys and ventilators, which looked like enormous chess pieces. Stairs led all over the roof, up and down, up and down, and then there were those incredible tiled shapes, some with crowns, others with crosses, others like knights with visors lowered over their faces.

It was a soft spring afternoon, even if my neck felt too exposed now to the breezes, and I leaned out over the roof thinking that this must be one of the most beautiful cities on earth.

And then I saw something very odd. Strolling down the Passeig de Gràcia, as comfortably as if it were Telegraph Avenue in Berkeley, was a woman whom I was positive had once given me a foot massage after a big march in San Francisco. It had been a couple of years ago when I'd been passing through on my way to a conference on Latin American women writers in Mexico City. I'd stopped to check my mail at Lucy's, renew my driver's license and get a pap smear, and Lucy had dragged me along with her to the march, where we strolled under the banner of her women's health clinic. At the end of the march we came to a park full of stands with political and fun things for sale, and there, sitting on a large quilt, with a velvet pillow and various creams and unguents around her, was a woman doing foot massage.

I couldn't resist; something about her drew me. Maybe it was her name and title—April Schauer, Foot Therapist—lettered in gold and indigo on a card, maybe it was the soulful expression in her midnight eyes. At any rate I sat myself down in front of her and put my foot on her well-upholstered lap, and let her look intensely into my eyes as she established instant intimacy with first my right foot and then my left. She was all velvet and fire, with kinky black hair, a large nose and a gorgeous full mouth, and she taught me what delicious feelings accrue in the soles once they are unshod.

"You have experienced feet," she told me and then I paid her seven dollars and we parted. Just one of life's many brief fascinating encounters. But here she was, I was sure it was her, walking down the Passeig de Gràcia, wearing a red velvet smock, a black shawl and Birkenstock sandals, and eating an ice cream cone. With amazement I watched her cross the street and disappear somewhere below me into the Provença entrance of La Pedrera.

It couldn't be anything but an odd coincidence, but still, the fact of the matter was that April had made an impression on me then and she still did. I suspected she was one of those holistic, earthy, goddess-types who probably liked to spend a lot of time in bed.

She couldn't—couldn't?—have any connection with Ben.

Frankie was in a much better mood when I met her at the Café de l'Opera on the Ramblas at seven-thirty. She noticed my haircut at once and demanded the name of my hairdresser. "Very chic," she said approvingly. "Much better than that awful turban."

"I'm not sure," I said. "I feel a little bit like a potted plant, with vines snaking over the sides of the pot."

She was looking pretty chic herself, in a neon green sheath dress with a tight black jacket. The dress was short enough to show her well-shaped, strong-looking legs in their black high heels. Her reddish curls were all over the place and her hazel eyes cheerfully outlined in green, black and a little silver. She was finishing a glass of red wine and munching on olives and looking quite at home in the old-fashioned café with its dark walnut tables and art nouveau wall panels.

I ordered a *fino* and gave her my report. I'd dropped the film off to be developed overnight, but described all the people I'd seen coming and going from La Pedrera. Nobody who looked anything like Ben.

"He couldn't be in disguise, could he?" I asked.

"I'll only know that when I see the photographs," she said noncommittally. "Do you think anyone noticed you?"

"I doubt it," I said. "I sat at the café outside for hours and worked on my translation." I didn't mention that I'd taken an hour off to see Carmen. "And then I went inside on the tour, up on the roof, just to get a feel for the layout of the building." That made me remember April.

"When I was on the roof I looked down and I thought I saw this woman who once gave me a foot massage in San Francisco."

Frankie gave a small start. Or was she just motioning to the waiter? "Another one," she said, pointing at her drink.

"What a coincidence," she smiled at me. "Are you sure?"

"She made an impression on me at the time," I admitted. "She thought I had experienced feet. She was pulling my big toe as she said it."

"It sounds more like she was pulling your leg," Frankie wrinkled her nose. I thought of warning her that a gamin habit acquired in your teens or twenties has a way of turning into irritating furrows in your forties, but what the hell, she'd find out for herself. "Now, back to business. I've changed hotels and I want you to meet me tomorrow morning after you've picked up the photos. We can go over them and then decide what to do next."

"Even for a hundred dollars a day I'm not willing to spend all my time staring at the door of La Pedrera," I complained. "And are you absolutely sure Ben is in Barcelona? The porter told me that no Americans are living in the building."

"I'm quite sure," she said. "And don't worry about your money." She took out an envelope and passed it to me. "It's in pesetas."

"Not here," I said. "Haven't I told you that Barcelona is a city of pickpockets? Especially down here on the lower part of the Ramblas and the streets off it. You shouldn't carry a lot of money around. I should have told you."

"I don't have a lot of money now," she giggled. "You do."

"I'm not kidding," I said. "Barcelona can be a dangerous place."

"Well, you'd better be careful then, hadn't you?" Frankie suddenly yawned and said, "I've got to get some sleep. See you tomorrow at the same place as this morning."

She gave me another bill and got up, making her way through the crowded, smoky café with a sway of her narrow hips and a confident toss of her auburn curls. A lot of people looked at her. A lot of men.

I noticed that one of them had a flight bag at his feet that read EUROPEAN SOCIETY FOR ORGAN TRANSPLANTATION. There must be a convention here this week.

4

I wasn't supposed to meet Ana at the restaurant until nine thirty, so after I finished my sherry at the Café de l'Opera I wandered out to the Ramblas again and into the Barri Gòtic. It was packed with people shopping and walking arm in arm through the narrow, brightly lit streets.

Then, in the bookstore window, I saw it.

A black-haired, lushly naked woman with a snake wrapped around her body and behind her a jungle straight from Henri Rousseau, though heavier on the parrots, monkeys and gardenias.

In the foreground was a young girl in a filmy white dress reclining on a sofa with a notebook in her hand and a rapt look upon her face. It was María the writer-daughter. It was Cristobel, *La Grande.* It was Gloria de los Angeles, winner of Venezuela's highest literary honors. It was, in short, the Spanish edition of *La Grande y su hija.*

I peeked in the door and saw readers eagerly poring over the first pages and taking it up to the cash register. A sign in the window said it was a publishing phenomenon, García Márquez in female form, the Venezuelan Allende, the biggest South American novel of the year!

And to think, I had the honor of being the English translator. I was even now walking through the streets of Barcelona with a notebook full of sentences like: "Night after night Cristobel snuck out into the velvet jungle to meet Eduardo, the only man who had ever, because she refused to count the forced

31

marriage of rapine caresses with Raoul, inflamed those soft loins. . . . " Or perhaps I should use "crept" instead of "snuck."

The South American edition of the book had been published in Buenos Aires and featured a woman and a man in a romantic but chaste embrace. Once that might have done for Spain as well, back in the old days when the censors used to carefully cut out women in bikinis from the European editions of *Time* and *Newsweek*. I felt in my cloth bag for *La Grande y su hija* in order to compare the two editions, and encountered a strange gaping hole and an absence of certain familiar objects—like the camera Frankie had bought for me and the cassette of Transylvanian Gregorian Chants.

Hell! I had gone into the ladies' toilet in the Café de l'Opera and carefully put Frankie's hundred dollars' worth of pesetas in my bra, but someone must have followed me out of the café and slit my bag in the crowd. The only thing left was my notebook, whose metal coils had caught on the fabric. They'd taken the novel, presumably thinking I'd put the envelope inside its pages.

I went into the bookstore and bought the last copy of the Spanish edition.

"You won't be able to put it down," the clerk assured me. "It will take over your imagination completely."

The seafood restaurant in the old fishing quarter of Barceloneta had tables outside, facing the Mediterranean, and the moon shone down on the waves and gave shape to their crashing voices.

"You sat and watched the door of La Pedrera all day?" demanded Ana. "That's more than we ever had to do as architectural students."

"Easy money," I defended myself. "I translated a good six pages just sitting there."

"I notice you made time for a new haircut," she said.

"I can always make time for a haircut from Carmen."

Ana snorted.

"*Calmete, mujer,*" I said. "Carmen has a heart of gold. Just think of her as being from a different country, that might help."

"Andalucía *is* a different country than Catalunya," Ana pointed out. "It was Franco who encouraged all the Andalucíans to come here, after the war. To make it more difficult to organize politically."

She waved over our waiter with an imperious hand. "They never learned Catalan, they refuse to learn Catalan. They don't want to be part of Catalunya."

"But I don't know Catalan," I said. "You talk to me in Spanish or English."

"You're different."

Ana rested her face on an elegant thin wrist and regarded me over our wine.

"I've missed you, Cassandra," she said. "It's been a long time."

"Well, not that long," I said cheerfully. "I see you more than I see some of my other friends. Natasha, for instance. Or Tomiko."

Ana did not like these sorts of references. "I've never understood," she said, "why you don't make Barcelona your base instead of London. You're a translator, you should be around the Spanish language. Of course you wouldn't want to live in South America, it's too dangerous. Or even Madrid. But Barcelona suits you."

It did suit me, no doubt about that, to sit outside in the moonlight by the shores of the Mediterranean and to drink Rioja with an attractive woman.

"Even if Barcelona were my base," I said carefully, "I still wouldn't be here much. You know me, I can't stay anywhere too long, I get crazy."

Our waiter brought the *paella,* fried to the darkness of mahogany. Peach-colored prawns and violet mussel shells decorated the top and the wonderful smell of saffron mixed with the night.

Ana poured me more wine.

"I like to travel too."

33

"No you do *not*, Ana. I mean, a trip to Rome or Paris for two weeks is not the same as a six-week trek through Mongolia."

"You're too old to keep this up, Cassandra. You need to settle down with someone, experience family life."

"Ana," I said, as gently as I could with my mouth full. "What *is* on your mind?"

"I've just been thinking about family," she said. "How I want one. I want children, I want a partner. It's almost getting too late for me to have a child."

"So have one. You can afford it. You can afford a nanny."

"But I don't want to do it alone." Ana stopped eating and looked at me with melting eyes. "And so I thought of all the people I would like to have a family with—and it came down to you, Cassandra."

I tried to keep it light, even though my instinctive reaction was to bolt for the sea.

"I'd be a terrible mother."

"No, you'd be wonderful. You're a fascinating woman, and you know a lot of languages, and you've been through a lot."

"But I don't like children all that much. I mean, I do. But not if they're my own."

"Well, it would be mine."

"I'll be its aunt, how about that?" I suggested. "I had a wonderful aunt myself," I said, and launched into a long story about Aunt Eavan who had singled me out from my six brothers and sisters and taken me to the theater in Chicago where she lived and given me a subscription to *National Geographic*.

"It was all those *National Geographics*, Ana. I realized that outside Kalamazoo there were thousands of bare-breasted women."

"I've always wondered why you started travelling," Ana said.

"Well, now you know, Ana. Now you know."

At about eleven-thirty we left the restaurant and walked out to where Ana had parked her Honda *moto*. It was a fine warm night and I said I wasn't quite ready to go home yet, that I wanted to walk a little.

Ana looked as if she were going to argue, but then gave in.

"You'll be able to get a taxi pretty easily when you're ready," she said, trying not to sound bossy. "I'll see you back home then, all right?"

I just smiled. I had no intention of telling her that I was meeting Carmen at a bar. I also had no intention of telling her that I planned to walk most of the way.

I hugged myself into my leather jacket and set off briskly. I made my way through the quiet streets of Barceloneta and crossed over the big avenues that separated the port of Barcelona from the Barri Gòtic. I thought I'd walk up Via Laietana, but halfway up was suddenly struck by the idea of seeing the cathedral at night and crossed into the twisting streets of the old quarter.

It was much darker down these streets, where the tall buildings squeezed out the sky and there were often no streetlights, only occasionally bright areas on the sidewalk from the bars. I tried to imagine that I was back in medieval Spain when the people passing me might be monks or troubadors. I listened to my steps on the stones, and kept turning down smaller and more deserted streets in order to get that feeling of centuries past.

I was so deeply in an imagined world that for a while I didn't realize I was being followed. I had thought the footsteps behind me were simply echoes. When I realized that someone was coming after me it was almost too late. I heard his labored breathing and his pounding feet. I didn't bother to glance around. I clutched my notebook and Gloria's novel and peeled out, dashing around corners and making for the cathedral square.

"Halt," I thought I heard him call out.

But I didn't feel like it.

◆

My desire for a midnight stroll having vanished, I took a cab the rest of the way to the bar. It was on a quiet street not far from Ana's apartment. At this hour on a weekday night it wasn't as crowded as usual, but I still had to fight my way in past gaggles of trendy young women with odd haircuts and beautiful clothes.

Up at the bar, talking with the bartender, was Carmen in skintight gold stretch pants and a wildly flowered overblouse. Her streaked hair was drawn into a French twist and she was smoking from a cigarette holder. The bartender looked interested.

"*Hola mujer,*" I said, sliding into place beside her.

She gave me a wet kiss and the bartender drifted innocently away.

"I was starting to wonder if you were really coming," she said, fluffing up my hair on top so that I was sure I looked like Medusa.

"What an evening I've had!" I told her about my sliced-open bag and about being followed near the cathedral.

But Carmen wasn't fazed. "Barcelona isn't a safe city," she said darkly. "I always carry a knife now."

"A knife! Carmen!" I wasn't surprised actually. Carmen was not a woman to cross, as one of her old girlfriends had discovered when she had started seeing someone else on the side. I don't like to say what happened; suffice it to say María Luisa currently feels more comfortable living in València.

Carmen called the bartender back and ordered me a drink. We pushed our way into a dimly lit corner of the room, near the writhing dance floor. Carmen put one hand on my thigh and other up the back of my shirt and we caught up on old times. I knew better than to suggest we go somewhere and continue our pleasures lying down. Because Carmen would suddenly remember that it was late and that her mother would be worried and that she had to get up early in the morning. As a heavy petter she had no equal, but if you liked to get horizontal you were out of luck with her. Horizontal meant sin. Vertical was just very very friendly.

Still, there was something I had to bring up with her. After about an hour of intense nuzzling I whispered, "Carmen, I have to tell you something."

"Yes, darling?"

"It's hard to tell you this."

"Tell me, darling."

"You won't be upset?"

"*Por favor, querida,* just say it."

"I'm not sure I like my new haircut."

She drew back in astonishment. Perhaps no one had ever said such a thing to her before.

"I mean," I said desperately, "it's beautiful, it's interesting, it's *chic*. But I'm not sure it's me."

Now she was insulted. "You're saying I don't know you?"

"Of course you do, but—"

"You're saying you want to go around wearing a turban your whole life?"

"A little more off the top, maybe. . . . " I pleaded.

She disengaged herself from me. "It's late," she said. "My mother will be worried. And I have to get up early tomorrow."

She marched out the door without a backward glance. No more snuggling tonight.

I would have to take matters into my own hands.

I let myself into the apartment and tiptoed through the rooms filled with everything from vacuum cleaner attachments to small golden Thai Buddhas, from sexually explicit African carvings to factory-size bolts of parachute cloth. I was relieved that Ana wasn't waiting up for me, as I'd half expected. For what I wanted to do I needed privacy.

I went into the big old-fashioned bathroom and locked the door. Carefully I took off my black jeans and Japanese shirt and wrapped myself in a towel so as not to get too cold. I took what I needed out of my cosmetic case and perched on the side of the tub in front of the full-length mirror. I didn't do it this way very often but that added to the excitement. I had a few goosebumps and I was perspiring lightly. The fantasy was very strong.

Slowly, very slowly, I raised the scissors to my crown and started snipping.

In fifteen minutes it was all over: I no longer looked like a potted plant, chic or not. In fact I looked rather like a religious figure from the Renaissance, I thought, my frizzy tendrils clipped to nubby curls next to my head.

If I'd had hair like this earlier this evening no man would have thought to chase me around the Barri Gòtic.

5

"Oh dear," said Frankie when she saw me late the next morning in the Plaça del Pi.

"Oh dear what?" I said good-naturedly. I had come ambling down the street, knife-proof leather briefcase containing the photos, my notebook and the adventures of *La Grande* dangling from my shoulder. I'd spent a productive few hours with María and Cristobel and was ready to revel in the warmth of the spring sunshine.

"I can never understand why some women want to look so... so masculine," she said.

"I cut my hair, that's all," I said. "I don't look masculine. I look like a middle-aged Irish-American Spanish translator with short hair."

She pursed her bright red lips, produced a cough from deep inside and lit a Camel. This woman smoked too much.

She changed the subject. "Did you get the photos?"

I tossed the packets on the table. "From the description you gave me," I said, "there's no one who looks like Ben."

"That remains to be seen," she said. She looked through all the photos carefully, and there must have been at least a hundred. At the end I'd cheated a little and taken pictures of obvious tourists.

"I'm not sure I can take another day of photography," I said. I didn't want to tell her that the expensive camera had been stolen from me yesterday.

"No, that won't be necessary," she said absent-mindedly.

She must have recognized someone. But who?

"What's the next step?" I asked.

Frankie put the photographs back in their envelopes and then put everything into a plastic purse the size of a small chair. "I don't think I'm going to need your services right now. I'd like to meet later, later this afternoon or early evening."

"And I'm just supposed to wait around Barcelona for you to decide how to use me next? Forget it," I said. "The deal was that I'd come to Barcelona and look for Ben for you and that I'd be paid whether or not I found him. Now you won't even tell me if I've found him or not."

"You'll get your money tomorrow," she said, and she didn't seem upset at all. "I've just got to think through the best way to deal with him."

"What are you going to do?" I asked.

"I'm going shopping," she said. "And I'd love the name of your hairdresser. Yesterday's hairdresser," she amended. "We can meet there at six o'clock."

I followed her, of course. She wandered up the Ramblas and through the Plaça de Catalunya, crossed the Ronda Universitat and strolled leisurely up the Rambla de Catalunya, looking as if she had all the time in the world. She dawdled in front of shoe stores and pastry shops, she went into boutiques and came out with parcels. At València she turned right towards the Passeig de Gràcia where she went even more slowly. It was driving me crazy watching her sashay along in her pointed shoes, taking small steps and swaying her hips slightly, glancing at her reflection in the windows that she passed, jangling her plastic bracelets and tossing her curls. All the same I had to admire her; it must be fun to enjoy your physical presence so much. Did she know I was following her? She seemed to be making her way towards La Pedrera. I decided to get there before she arrived and so crossed the Passeig de Gràcia and walked quickly in the direction of Provença. Just as I reached La Pedrera I saw two kids, a muscular adolescent boy and what looked like his younger sister, come out of the building and head towards me. They weren't alone; they were accompanied by April Schauer, foot therapist, in a cream-colored caftan with raspberry and peach silk scarves around her neck and long silver earrings. What a gorgeous woman! I glanced across the wide boulevard but Frankie seemed as lazily oblivious as before, pausing now in front of another shop.

I suppose I should have continued to follow her, but on the spur of the moment I decided to go after April instead. There was more than a coincidence here, I was sure of it.

Within a block April and the two kids vanished into a subway station. I raced after them and tailed them onto the green line. I thought it extremely unlikely that April would recognize me, but I kept my dark glasses on and my feet tucked securely under the seat.

I couldn't keep my eyes off April, that gypsy with her braided leather bracelets and silver bells around her fat ankles. Were they her kids? The little girl was about six or seven, plain and unremarkable in a short dress and pigtails. The boy had a blond brush cut and was wearing a vest, jeans and Converse high-top sneakers. He was well developed for a youngster, his biceps visible under the rolled-up sleeves of his tee-shirt. He was probably about sixteen—but then I really looked at him and saw I'd made a serious mistake.

High Tops was very much a girl, in fact, a woman, in fact she looked suddenly very much like someone you'd see pitching at a softball game in San Francisco. Once I realized that, I couldn't understand how I'd been mistaken. The woman had breasts, for christssakes, and a rhinestone stud in one ear, and small hands and feet. It was true she didn't look like most of the women wandering around Barcelona, but she was still recognizably a woman.

I was still in shock when they got off at Lesseps and started off in the direction of Gaudí's Parc Güell. April and High Tops were deep in some discussion and the little girl dragged her feet behind them.

After a twenty-minute walk we all arrived at the entrance to Parc Güell, where the blue-and-white-checked undulating tower with the double cross stood across from the porter's lodge with its billowing crown of creamy tile and bright mosaics. I supposed that April and High Tops had been here before, perhaps many times, for they scarcely gave the two gingerbread houses a second glance, and immediately began to climb the staircase up to the plaza. But the little girl was charmed and delighted by it all. She stopped on the staircase to marvel at the fountain shaped like a big blue lizard and again to stare at the huge columns supporting the square.

It was a pretty wild place, the Parc Güell—a cross between a surreal Disneyland and a Max Ernst painting. Gaudí and his patron Güell had once had enormous visionary plans for this site. It was to have been a garden-city high on a hill overlooking Barcelona, with all sorts of amazing houses and vegetation. But the only houses that had been built were Gaudí's and Güell's, and the forest of pillars that held up the plaza, meant to be a porticoed marketplace, had never seen a vendor.

Up on the plaza, scalloped by a winding bench made from broken polychromed ceramics, the view was splendid and vast. The city shimmered in a haze of spring warmth and beyond it the azure Mediterranean promised voyages to distant countries. For a moment I was tempted to abandon this idiotic job and rush down to the offices of the Balearic lines and book a passage to Palma or Ibiza. Then I saw that April and High Tops had found a seat in one of the curves of the serpentine ceramic bench and were unpacking a picnic lunch. I sat down nearby and took out *La Grande y su hija,* opened it near the beginning and read:

It was the year that most of the population of my village vanished. The young people were the first to go, and at first no one thought it odd: from time immemorial boys had run off to join the circus or the army, girls had joined sweethearts or disappeared to hide the shame of pregnancy. So in the beginning no one paid any attention. But then Pablo Ruíz did not open up his toyshop one morning; and the following week the mayor did not appear in the town square to dedicate the new fountain (which had caused a great scandal when first proposed because of the suggestive draperies of the Botticelli-like Venus). The school eventually closed because first one and then another and finally the third teacher did not appear for class, and sick people grew sicker and often died because the doctor no longer came to his clinic. Babies went without food and lovers without caresses; those who lived for their hatreds found no one left to quarrel with.

Eventually the situation became so bad that those who remained in the village had nothing to eat and no one to eat it with. And those few remaining survivors of the mysterious disappearing plague packed up their possessions and fled.

At first the conversation I overheard was not particularly illuminating. It went something like this:

High Tops: Delilah, I've got a chicken sandwich and a cheese sandwich. Which would you like?

Delilah: I'm not hungry.

High Tops: Oh of course you are. It's way past noon.

April: Children need to develop spontaneous eating habits. If they're forced they—

Delilah: I want to go play!

High Tops: Oh all right. But then you have to come back and eat something.

[Pause, while Delilah runs off and joins Spanish children kicking a very small ball around.]

April: Don't you find it hard to be a mother?

High Tops: Oh April, let's not talk about that again. I love you so much, baby, I can't stand the thought of not being with you.

April [sighing]: I love you too, sweetheart. But there are so many complications.

High Tops: Oh don't worry about him.

April: It's not that I'm worried, but—

High Tops: Honey, I've done everything I can and I'll keep doing everything I can to be near you.

High Tops had forgotten all about Delilah and her lunch and was completely focused on April. Her squarish, rather plain face was illuminated by romantic yearning, and she stroked April's shoulders and back as April polished off two sandwiches and an apple. In her cream caftan April looked like a Bedouin queen; I could see why High Tops was enamored. Yes, that I understood. But I didn't understand any of the rest of it. Did these two and Delilah have any connection to Ben and Frankie? Was Ben the "him" not to be worried about?

In a desultory way I read the same paragraph of *La Grande* over and over:

My mother loved Eduardo with a passion like music, a full symphony that comes, after years of silence, to one in solitary confinement. Eduardo had been predicted long ago, while Cristobel was still married to Raoul, on a sultry day down by the river, when an old gypsy had taken her hand and said, "You will find great love, but never fulfillment." Cristobel snatched her hand away. "It can't be great love then." The gypsy had gazed with enormous sympathy at Cristobel before entering the river and submerging herself in the transparent silver-green eddies. "How little you know about love," she had said, before the river covered her and bore her along.

The afternoon was heating up and I was tired. I had missed my own lunch by now and hadn't dared even stop for a mineral water at the bar for fear of losing them. I was becoming extremely cranky and planning how I would take it out on Frankie when I met her later. Then things began to get more interesting.

April and High Tops had stopped talking some time ago and were merely keeping half an eye on Delilah as they lolled in the sun. I'd gotten up for just a minute to walk and stretch myself and had immediately lost my seat to yet another tourist with a flight bag reading EUROPEAN SOCIETY FOR ORGAN TRANS-PLANTATION. Now I was restlessly wandering out of hearing distance with Gloria de los Angeles's bestseller under my arm. Suddenly I noticed that High Tops was barefoot and had her right foot in April's lap. I wished it could have been me. Or perhaps not, because obviously the public practice of Reflexol-ogy was not usual in Spain, and April and High Tops soon be-gan to excite a disquieted interest among the other visitors to the plaza. Well, it did look pretty erotic. April had her serpent eyes fastened on High Tops' stubby white foot as if it were a morsel she was about to strike and swallow whole. High Tops had flung her shoulders back in a pose of great abandonment and was groaning in a manner not particularly suited to public places.

The situation was ripe for chastisement, and if the police had happened by, High Tops and April might have been forced to re-shoe and desist, but instead, a youngish man walked up casu-ally to them and starting talking in English.

Medium height, regular-looking, wearing jeans. It was Ben. It must be Ben. If I were describing him I would have thought to mention that he was quite good-looking, in spite of a reced-ing hairline and a tendency to plumpness around the middle. He didn't look particularly dangerous, nor did April and High Tops seem at all alarmed to see him. They greeted him warmly and then both exclaimed in great surprise. Something had hap-pened that they wanted to hear about. Was it Frankie's arrival in Barcelona?

I pretended that a certain mosaic pattern near them was in-tensely fascinating to me, but I was afraid to get too close. As a result I heard only fragments of their conversation.

Ben: . . . Going to Barcelona wasn't part of the agreement. She's angry.

April: . . . No right to be angry. . . It's not as if. . .

High Tops: . . . absolutely impossible to discuss. . .

Ben: They're her feelings.

They must be talking about Frankie. Her feelings. She's angry. Then Ben knew Frankie was in Barcelona. Frankie had gone to see him at La Pedrera after I took off after April and High Tops. My job was over. But why did I feel so uneasy?

I wondered what the papers were that Frankie wanted Ben to sign, and whether he had come to Barcelona to avoid Frankie rather than just for a visit. I wondered how April and High Tops knew Ben and whether they also knew Frankie. I wondered why April and High Tops had mentioned being worried about Ben but were now treating him in a perfectly friendly, even confidential way.

But it had become too hot for speculation. I didn't have an interest in getting much more involved. All I wanted was my money and to say good-bye to Frankie.

I spent the rest of the afternoon working on *La Grande y su hija* back at Ana's. Ana was absorbed in her seashell house and with her usual single-minded intensity was affixing a mosaic of real shells all around its opening. I wondered what it would be like to have Ana make a house for me.

"Wouldn't you like a room like a nun's?" she asked.

"Are you kidding? A hard single bed with a crucifix above it?"

"But your life is so complicated, Cassandra, you live in so many places. Think if you had a little white room with a painting of the sea, a room you could always return to."

"You're talking to an Irish Catholic girl who grew up in a little white room and couldn't wait to get out of it."

Ana shook her head. "But that room is still your center. You need that room."

"And where might this room be, might I ask?"

"Why, right here in my apartment," she said. "Next to the nursery."

◆

I waited until after six to meet Frankie at Carmen's salon. For a minute I thought of donning my turban again, but in the end decided to brave it. So what if Carmen had a knife? I had taken karate for six weeks. And in Kyoto, too.

But Frankie wasn't there when I arrived and I had to face Carmen's wrath alone.

"Ay, ay, ay!" she screamed. "Where is it? Where's your hair? Yesterday you had too much. Now you have none."

"It will grow back," I promised.

"Where did you go? Who did this butchering job? I will kill her."

I admitted that I'd done it myself and she screamed again, as if I'd confessed to performing an appendectomy on my own body.

"But why? You were beautiful with my haircut. Now you're ugly. Ugly. Ugly!" She grabbed my arm and shoved me in front of one of the mirrors.

I thought I looked rather handsome.

"Your beautiful curls," she moaned. "I can't bear it."

But at that moment Frankie entered and Carmen was diverted.

"This is Frankie," I introduced them. "Carmen."

Carmen gave a sharp intake of breath, and I thought she was probably jealous, no doubt imagining that Frankie and I had a relationship beyond that of client and investigator.

Frankie bussed me on the cheek. "I've had *such* a successful day," she enthused.

"Yes?"

"I found some absolutely fabulous clothes. Terribly *European.*"

She sat down in the chair and I wondered what she thought Carmen could do for her. Those corkscrew auburn curls looked perfectly wonderful to me.

"Take it off, darling," she said in English to Carmen with a wave.

And Carmen did.

I gasped.

"You mean you didn't know it was a wig, Cassandra?" Frankie said to me in the mirror. "That's wonderful."

The woman in the mirror looked completely different. She had chin-length limp hair that had been forced to change color once too often and was now an unprepossessing shade of burnt toast. The wig had made Frankie's features pretty; without it her chin was too sharp, her nose too big, her eyes too small.

But as an actress she must be used to changing her appearance all the time, and to think nothing of it.

"Don't cut off too much, darling," Frankie told Carmen. "I like it as full as you can make it."

I translated, minus the *darling*, as Carmen picked up an over-processed lock and let it drop significantly before brusquely pointing to the wash basins.

"When you said you had a successful day, I thought it was because you'd met with Ben finally," I said while she was being shampooed.

"Ben?"

"I saw you go into La Pedrera just after... two women and a little girl came out. I followed them to the Parc Güell and heard all about you."

Frankie blanched slightly. But it could have been Carmen energetically scrubbing at the roots of her hair.

"And then I saw Ben come up to the two women and—"

"Ben came up to the two women?" Frankie repeated.

"Well, obviously Ben is staying with them and their little girl."

Frankie yelped in pain. "Not—so—hard. *Por favor.*"

"Well, isn't he?" I demanded.

"Yes." Frankie sighed.

I followed them back to the styling chair. Carmen looked grim, I supposed because we were talking in English and Frankie was treating her like a hairdresser. She hated that.

"And you met with Ben today, didn't you?"

Frankie pondered this while looking at her sallow complexion in the mirror. "Yes, briefly."

"Well, you've gotten what you came for, haven't you?"

"Not exactly." Her eyes followed Carmen's scissors closely. "You see, I couldn't get him to sign the papers. I'll have to do a little more persuading."

"But my part in all this is finished."

"I might need a little help persuading—"

"Absolutely not."

"All I want you to do is sit near us at a restaurant tomorrow. When the time is right I'll introduce you."

"Well . . . "

"And then I'll give you your check for two thousand plus today's and tomorrow's expenses and you can be on your way."

"I'll think about it," I said moodily. But we both knew I'd help her out yet again.

Carmen was blow-drying Frankie's hair. She hadn't done a bad job with the cutting—Carmen would never do a bad job—but neither had she thrown herself into it. Frankie seemed too distracted to notice.

"So you followed the two women, hmmm?" she asked. "Where did you say they went?"

"To the Parc Güell. It looks like they probably eat their lunch there regularly. And that's where Ben joined them."

"I've heard of that park," said Frankie. "I hope I can sightsee a little while I'm here."

Carmen stood back and handed Frankie a mirror so she could check the back of her head. It was a nice style job, if you liked pageboys. I knew Carmen didn't.

"Thank you dear," Frankie said indifferently as she got out her red purse.

"You pay the cashier," I whispered, as Carmen's eyes smouldered at this final insult. She flicked the towel off Frankie's shoulders as if it were a bullfighter's cape.

I accompanied Frankie to the door.

"Cassandra," Carmen called sternly after me. "Can we talk a minute?"

"I'm late to meet Ana," I said, hoping to avoid another lecture, this time on American manners. "Can you call me to-night?"

She raised her eyebrows. "I suppose it's not *that* important."

I've never lost my nerve when it really counted, but I'm a complete coward when it comes to facing an angry woman. As usual, I escaped.

6

It had all started, Ana said that evening after dinner, when a newly pregnant client came to her and requested a house for herself, so that she could lie in it and think maternal thoughts. Ana at first thought of it as something of a challenge, because she had never been pregnant. A thorough researcher, Ana went to the library and bookstores and obtained big tomes on pregnancy and childbirth, complete with full-color photographs.

She was fascinated by the thought of a house that grew, month by month, and at the beginning investigated pliable construction materials into which could be pumped air or water. There was even a point at which she envisioned the house as a giant amniotic sac in which the woman could float like a fish in an aquarium. However, like all architects, even of miniature houses, Ana had to reckon with the conservatism and impatience of her client.

She wasn't going to be pregnant forever, the woman reminded Ana.

So Ana had come up with a bright papier-mâché shell in the shape of a woman with a big belly and huge, wide-spread legs. The entrance was between the legs and the interior was fitted out with a foam mattress covered in rose velvet. There was a little skylight in the belly button, and a tape recorder in the head that played gentle pop music.

"But all that reading about pregnancy and childbirth had

done something to me," said Ana. "I'm thirty-five and I've been constructing children's houses for ten years. Am I never going to have a child of my own?"

"I thought you said you got what you needed from making children happy with their houses?"

"I *used* to," said Ana, absently stroking her flat belly. "But all those books awakened deep-seated feelings. Strange maternal feelings. On the streets I sought out pregnant women and stared at them, I haunted maternity clothes shops, I even arranged with a doctor friend of mine to be present at a birth in the hospital."

"I think you should just go ahead and have a child," I said.

"I couldn't raise a child alone."

"Of course you can. My mother raised us alone. Not that we turned out very well, but still."

"I don't *want* to raise a child alone."

"I don't like the way you're looking at me, Ana."

"You'd be perfect, Cassandra. Intelligent, cultured, humorous and active."

"You skipped warm, accepting and reliable. Probably because you know me."

"The point is, I don't know anybody else I could possibly consider."

"Well, at least that takes it out of the realm of the personal. I don't have to worry that it's only *me* who will do."

Ana had one of her sudden fits of temper. They always came upon her like an allergic reaction. Her pale face turned blazing red, her dark eyes grew enormous and hard. "Yes, laugh at me, that's right. I'm trying to tell you something important, but just go ahead, laugh at me!"

"Ana, Ana, calm down. I just meant—"

"Yes, I know exactly what you meant. You don't want to have anything to do with me!" she wailed. "And you're my one hope."

"Ana," I said. "You're not even attracted to me."

As suddenly as it had begun her temper tantrum abated. She

got up and cleared off the table. "My god," she said. "You know, that's true."

She looked me over critically. "Especially with that haircut."

I slept in the next morning and was awakened by an energetic-sounding Frankie, who told me that Ben had agreed to meet her at a restaurant in the Plaça Reial at one o'clock. If I could come then too and order myself lunch, Frankie would signal me when the time was right to join them. All she wanted was my presence at the table, she emphasized. Ben was always better behaved when there were other people around.

I supposed Frankie had chosen the Plaça Reial because it was such an obvious tourist spot. What the tourists rarely realized was that the formal plaza with its arcades and palms, its fountain of the Three Graces in the center, was a hang-out for drug dealers and pickpockets. There used to be a Thieves Market in the corner of the plaza but the police had put a stop to it by parking their own van there. Still, the square was still not a place to go by yourself at night.

During the day it was filled with tourists, who congregated especially at the outdoor bars and restaurants facing the sun. I didn't see either Ben or Frankie so I sat down at an empty table and took out my notebook and my copy of *La Grande y su hija*.

I was pleased that I was making progress on Cristobel's adventures even in the midst of my own. At this rate I would be done with the translation before my deadline and out of London, with my three thousand dollars from Frankie, before the end of May. I had in mind to visit friends in Eastern Europe and see how they were surviving the political changes of recent years. It was time to brush up on my Romanian, which I hadn't had much use for since a rather uncomfortable incident in Bucharest with a black marketeer and a member of the secret police.

Thus occupied with dreamy thoughts I almost didn't notice Ben cross the plaza and take a table right next to me. Bugger.

Would this be too close? Frankie could hardly remark, Oh look, there's my friend Cassandra, about a woman seated right next to them. But there was nothing to be done about it. I buried my face behind the jungle green nakedness of the novel and hoped for the best.

Ben looked as out of place as I felt. He was wearing jeans again and a striped Oxford shirt, but somehow he looked less American than he had yesterday at the Parc Güell. Perhaps it was just the proximity to real Americans. Perhaps it was the gold hoop in his ear or the blue ostrich leather boots. If Frankie had chosen this place because she thought we'd blend in, she was mistaken.

The waiter came over. "*Señor?*"

I looked around and realized he was talking to me. I quickly ordered the menu of the day. I began with an *ensalada de tomates*, followed by a *tortilla español* and then roast chicken. Afterwards I'd have a flan perhaps, and coffee. I thought I might need all three courses if Frankie didn't show up soon.

Even though we were outside, the noise among the tables was deafening. Maybe there was a tour group here enjoying a taste of the real Barcelona. Women in pantsuits with strong midwestern accents and pink and blue hair talked about how they just loved this Gaudy architecture, while their husbands discussed bullfights and how many miles they'd covered that day. Young couples carrying *The Rough Guide to Europe* or Frommer's *Spain on $40 a Day* (hadn't it once been five dollars a day?) argued about whether they could fit in Seville before Madrid or whether two days in Granada was too much.

I read a few pages of *La Grande* but I couldn't help eavesdropping on the conversation of two college-aged women nearby. They had obviously just met and were trading horror stories about the French.

"They might as well have put their hands over their ears when I asked them a question. It was that blatant!"

"You'd think they thought of French as some kind of sacred holy language. It's just a *language* for pete's sake."

"Boy, I never was so glad to get out of a country in my *life*. I like Barcelona. The Spanish seem really friendly."

"Oh, I think so too. I met the cutest guy at my hotel. He *wanted* to talk English with me."

Then a most awkward thing happened.

"Isn't that a great novel?"

I jumped. It was Ben, smiling disarmingly and pointing to the book in my hand.

I put on my best Irish accent. "Well and it's certainly a vivid picture of life in South America today. From a woman's point of view of course."

"That's what I thought," Ben said, leaning closer. "I mean, we've been hearing from García Márquez and Donoso and Vargas Llosa for years. But what about the women?"

Oh god, he was a feminist type of guy. And he knew about South American writers.

"May I join you?" he said, convinced that we had a lot in common. "I'm waiting for a friend, but she hasn't shown up yet. I can't stand eating by myself, it really makes me lose my appetite, especially in a place like this."

Curiosity has always been my downfall. I invited Ben to sit down with a wave of my hand. Frankie would just have to lump it.

"I'm Hamilton Kincaid," he said, holding out a firm brown hand. "Originally from New York, but I've been living in Barcelona for the last few years." He had blue eyes and a couple of days' growth of blond beard.

If he wanted to bluff it so could I. "Brigid O'Shaughnessy," I said. "From Dublin."

"That name sounds familiar somehow," he said.

"I'm a journalist."

"I don't read newspapers much," he apologized. "I try to keep up with contemporary fiction—Eco, Kundera, the Latin Americans, naturally—but I always feel I'm behind. Of course I try to read literature in the original and that takes a bit longer."

"What do you do?" I asked him. Besides try to impress girls like me?

"Oh, I play a little music. Saxophone."

Dilettante. I smiled charmingly. "So you think you've been stood up?"

"She said one and it's one-thirty. But then my friend is—how shall I put it?—something of a free spirit."

Strange that Frankie had said the same about him. Just a couple of free spirits with hidden agendas.

"Is she Spanish?"

"No, she's another American. It's her first visit to Spain."

"Oh dear, and you've been cajoled into playing tour guide."

"Not exactly," Ben sighed, and broke off a piece of bread. "I just met her yesterday. I never would have guessed."

"Guessed what?"

"That she was transsexual. . . . Do you know any transsexuals?"

Now that you mention it, I guess I did. A dozen details about Frankie flashed through my head and reorganized themselves.

Ben went on quickly. "Not that I'm judgmental. People are different. I'm gay for instance."

He misinterpreted my stunned silence and apologized. "I'm sorry. Being from Ireland, you're probably not used to talking about homosexuals, much less transsexuals."

"You'd be surprised," I managed with a wan smile. "We Catholics love to dress up."

The waiter brought our salads over and I had another surprise. Ben spoke to him in quite credible Catalan. There was something I didn't understand going on here. If Ben had only recently arrived from San Francisco, how on earth could he have picked up Catalan? Spanish he might have studied at school. But Catalan?

"So Brigid," he said, pouring me a glass of wine from the carafe. "What brings you to Barcelona?"

I told him that I was doing a piece for the *Irish Times* on how Barcelona was preparing for the 1992 Olympic Games, while all the time my mind was reeling in confusion.

If Frankie was a transsexual then Ben could hardly be her ex-husband.

Unless Ben had married Frankie thinking she was a woman.

Perhaps Frankie was blackmailing Ben, threatening to tell his family that he'd been married to a transsexual.

But if Ben were gay why would he have married Frankie in the first place?

Why had Ben said he only met Frankie yesterday?

And just where was Frankie anyway?

Our first course was taken away and our second course and our third course put before us, but still there was no sign of Frankie. It was now two o'clock and Ben was telling me about how he'd come to Barcelona because of the jazz scene. Some of the best musicians in Europe had congregated here, at places like the Harlem Club and the Cova del Drac.

The more details he gave the more worried I got. It sounded more and more as if he really did live in Barcelona. And if he lived in Barcelona and lived at La Pedrera, then it was likely that High Tops, Delilah and April Schauer were visiting him and not the other way around.

"I keep thinking you look familiar," I finally said. "And now I remember where I saw you. Yesterday, at the Parc Güell. You were with two women and a little girl."

Ben shot me a rather strange look, as if it had occurred to him for the first time that he had reason to be on guard with a stranger. "Yes," he said finally. "I usually go there around this time of day. I like to eat my lunch outside. It's a place I showed to some friends who are visiting. I usually meet them there around this time—"

He broke off suddenly, and stared at me.

"Excuse me," he said. "I've just remembered something."

He threw down a thousand pesetas and rushed across the square.

I threw down another thousand and followed him. The thought had probably come to both of us simultaneously that if Frankie wasn't here, she might well be at the Parc Güell. Only Ben knew why.

He was nowhere to be seen when I came dashing out of the Plaça Reial onto the Ramblas. I quickly hailed a cab. Would I get there before him, and if so, what would I find?

Twenty minutes later I arrived at the Parc Güell and rushed breathlessly through the portals, up past the blue lizard fountain to the plaza supported on wide pillars. There was no sign of Frankie, no sign either of High Tops, Delilah and April. I came back down the stairs and looked between the pillars. Nothing.

It was a warm afternoon and I had gotten myself in a sweat with my haste and alarm. I'd been trying to remember the pronouns April and High Tops had used when talking yesterday. When they'd talked about being worried they'd said "he," hadn't they? But when Ben had joined them they'd talked about a "she." Ben had said "she" in the restaurant.

I set off along the Passeig de las Palmeras, up the road that wound itself around the hillside. Unlike the Doric columns that supported the plaza, the columns underneath me now were a forest of wildly tilted trees, encrusted with dusty brown stones. The crazy thing about Gaudí was that his structures were so absolutely sound, perfect parabolas capable of bearing enormous weight, and yet his surfaces were so irregular. They gave the appearance of being natural, of having been part of the planet for millenia, and at the same time looked completely new, completely unlike anything you'd seen before.

Above the parabolic brown forest the road progressed in a stately, if precipitous, fashion around the curve of the spring green hill. At regular intervals were vast columns that held up nothing but the sky, rocks bleached a pinkish brown, great columns that resembled women marching slowly upwards with gargantuan baskets of fruits and vegetables on their heads, or a religious procession. The Festival of the Cacti, one could almost call it, for from the planters balanced on the columns spewed blades and spears, green-gray, desert-dry.

There were grandmothers in black with children, resting on the benches set into the railing along the edge of the road, the railing airily pieced together from sharp rocks; there were tourists sweating with cameras and guidebooks, in sturdy shoes and sleeveless shirts. Finally I reached the top of the hill and, turning a corner, saw the three of them. April, High Tops and Delilah were seated on a bench in the shade. Even from a distance I could see that High Tops looked shaken, April serene and Delilah merely apathetic and tired. I was wondering whether to go up to them and say something (could I possibly remind April that she'd once rubbed my soles?), when I heard the sound of running behind me.

"You!" said Ben, astonished. Then he saw them ahead of us off the road.

"Hamilton," said April dramatically. "You'll never guess what almost happened!"

"Where have you been, Hamilton?" asked High Tops. "He never would have tried anything if you had been here."

Hamilton shook his head irritably.

"This is Brigid O'Shaughnessy," he said. "And I think she knows more than she's let on."

"Well, actually," I said, "I think I'm more in the dark than any of you."

"Let's begin at the beginning," April said. "I'm April Schauer."

"I know," I said. "You massaged my feet once."

"I did?" She seemed pleased. "You remembered me from that?"

"April," High Tops said. "This woman's name is not Brigid O'Shaughnessy. Not unless mine is Sam Spade."

"I'm Cassandra Reilly," I admitted. "And who are you?"

"Me?" she said, as if surprised I had to ask. "I'm Ben."

7

Delilah was not a particularly attractive child, but small and spindly, with fair fine hair through which you could see her scalp, as fresh as a melon. Her ears were too large and when she grew up she would probably try to hide them, just as she would most likely adopt bangs to disguise the tall slant of her forehead. She wore her glasses as a child wears glasses, warily and resignedly. At six years old she already had the look of a child who has learned to be adaptable.

Unlike the young children of my friends in London who sported six earrings in each ear and tee-shirts that said "Save the Rainforest," Delilah was in a dress and sneakers. She wasn't wearing any jewelry at all, nor did she have a slogan on her skinny little chest, and you had the feeling that was her idea.

"What happened, honey?" Hamilton asked her. He crouched down to her level and put his brown hands on her small shoulders.

She sighed and scuffed her foot in the dry earth. "Frankie came up and told me that if I'd go with her I'd get some ice cream. She said we'd go off and get ice cream for everybody and come back and surprise Ben and April. I said okay and we started to go off but then Ben saw us and started screaming, so Frankie took off."

Delilah looked at Ben. "How come Frankie is here in Spain? Did he come to visit us?"

"Yes, Delilah. He came to visit us," Ben said. She looked exhausted and worried.

"Why did you scream at him?"

"Uhmm, I guess because it looked like you might be going away without telling us where you were going. We didn't mean to scare him."

"Maybe she just wanted to see Delilah," suggested Hamilton. After all, she's her father."

"He sees Delilah regularly in San Francisco. There's no reason he had to follow us on our vacation."

I was having some trouble following the pronouns. To Hamilton Frankie was a she, to Ben a he; Delilah used both depending on who she was talking to.

"And just where do you fit in?" April asked me suddenly. She was as intensely attractive as I remembered her. Her eyelids were dusky violet and her lips a natural rose. Crystal pendants and embroidered cloth bags hung around her neck and down into the brown cleavage visible under her silky blue shirt, and she gave off a scent that conjured up rich dark Biblical words like frankincense and myrrh.

"Well, I got a call from Frankie in London where I live saying she... he knew a friend of mine and wanted my help finding her... his ex-husband, Ben, and she'd pay my expenses and a fee for finding him... her. Frankie didn't say anything about a child. Of course he... she didn't say she was transsexual." I gave up on the pronouns. "Frankie said Frankie was married, had been married to a gay man named Ben, who was very wealthy and had just left town. The family needed some papers signed. That's why Frankie was looking for Ben. I thought Hamilton was Ben actually. You have to admit, Ben's not exactly common name for a woman."

"Short for Bernadette," she sighed.

"Well, all I can say is I'm sorry if I've made more problems for you."

"You've lost your Irish accent," Hamilton noted with a frown.

"So you were working for Frankie, and he paid you to find me," said Ben.

"Frankie paid part of my fee," I allowed, with the sinking feeling that I was probably never going to see the rest of it. "How was I to know? It sounded plausible, at least at the beginning. I never expected anything like this. I never heard of anything like this. Have I been away from the States too long?"

April said, "Hamilton, maybe Delilah would like to take a walk."

"Yes!" said Delilah.

They set off back down the slope of Max Ernst pillars, Hamilton with a slight avuncular stoop that suggested he was used to children, Delilah skipping in her dress.

I turned to Ben. Up close this woman was even more brawnily daunting. Her biceps bulged, her deltoids distended, her pectorals protruded underneath her sleeveless tee-shirt and vest. I supposed that April, as a masseuse, was attracted to such a display of well-defined musculature. It must be of great physiological interest.

"I don't know what to do," she said. "It can't go on like this. He's determined to kidnap Delilah, I know he is."

The three of us sat down on a stone bench, and Ben took April's round arm into her lap. She seemed unable to keep her hands off her girlfriend.

"Do you know *any* of the background of all this?" Ben asked. "Did Frankie tell you *anything*?"

"I'm at a loss," I admitted. "Are you married to Frankie? Were you married? Is Delilah your child?"

"She's *my* child," said Ben with some ferocity. "That's the problem. Frankie's trying to steal her."

April murmured in a placating tone, "Ben, remember that Frankie sees things differently."

"I gather you had Delilah... together, then," I said, searching for the right words. "Before Frankie... umm... changed."

"We were *pals*," Ben said, squeezing April's arm sadly. "It wasn't supposed to be like this. We knew each other in college, in the theater department. We dreamed of San Francisco, and we moved there right after graduation—we were going to stick together and make it."

April tried to remove her arm from Ben's grasp, but Ben only clung to her more firmly. "Yes, we got married, I got pregnant. What did we know? We were from Iowa. I had Delilah and then I got a job at Federal Express and Frankie started working as a waiter. I come to find out it's a bar with female impersonators and that he's been doing impersonation himself."

"It's a valid art form, Ben," April said. "It's as old as civilization."

"I'm not naive," Ben protested. "Okay, so people are different. So why should I be upset when Frankie comes to me and says he's always felt more like a girl than a boy, that he's never wanted to be macho. So he was a fag, well, I guess I always *knew* that. Just like I knew I wasn't like the girls I knew growing up. But I'm still a goddamned woman!"

"Ben, Ben," April said, withdrawing her arm firmly. "You said you were going to work on your attitude. Frankie is still a child of the Goddess."

"Oh honey, don't be mad. I love you so much. But don't you understand, I'm not against Delilah having a father. I'm not a separatist or anything. But Frankie is fucking trying to usurp my biological role!"

I tried to get back to the story. "So you and Frankie had a baby and then Frankie had a sex change. You have joint custody of Delilah, right?"

Ben nodded.

"I have her during the week and Frankie has her on the weekends. But on the weekends Frankie works at this club, as a cocktail waitress. He makes Delilah sit in the entertainers' dressing room for hours. Is that any place for a child?"

I supposed it wasn't appropriate to say that it sounded more fun than going to bed early Saturday night with your hair in big scratchy rollers, so you could get up at dawn for mass the next morning. That was how I'd spent my childhood.

"We were arguing all the time," Ben said. "When I com-

64

plained about his work he said he'd take Delilah during the week, and I could have her on the weekends. I couldn't agree to that. Finally I just couldn't stand him anymore. I had to get away for awhile. Take a vacation. But now he's followed us."

"So what are you going to do?"

Ben fixed me with her blue Iowa eyes. "Can't you help, Cassandra? I mean, after all, you have some responsibility. You led Frankie to us. Can't you persuade him that we're just here for a vacation? It's *so* important for April and me to be together right now."

"You *are* planning to go back, then?"

"Of course. It's just a couple of weeks. If Frankie would just go home and relax we could sort it all out then."

There was no denying that I had helped Frankie locate them, and that I probably did bear some responsibility. However, it wasn't guilt that made me agree to look for Frankie now and talk to her; it was indignation at having been used. And, I admit, some curiosity.

But finding Frankie might not be the easiest task in the world.

Leaving Ben and April in the Parc Güell, I gave in to the midday heat and took a taxi back to the Ramblas, to the posh hotel where Frankie had told me she was staying.

They said they didn't have a guest by that name.

I described her first as a curly redhead and then as a brunette with a pageboy. I even tried describing her as a man. The desk clerk gave me a strange look and grew more adamant. No one like that had been a guest in this hotel.

I wondered if Frankie had given me the wrong hotel by mistake. There were several three-star hotels along the Ramblas and I asked at each one, each time with the same results. No redheads, no brunettes and no men by the name of Frankie Stevens had ever checked in or out.

It was about five when I sat down in the *xoclateria*, the chocolate café off the Plaça del Pi, to consider what to do. I'm too trusting, perhaps, but it irked me to have been so thoroughly misled. Maybe Frankie did want Delilah back, but was that any reason to spin a story about a gay ex-husband and lead me to Barcelona to do her leg work for her? She'd clearly never meant to confront Ben and April directly, but to use me to get to them. And what about Hamilton? Who was he and why were April and Ben staying with him? Why had Frankie gone through Hamilton? She'd met with him yesterday and arranged to meet with him today at lunch. But all she'd wanted was to make sure he wasn't with April and Ben when she kidnapped Delilah.

And now Frankie had vanished. Maybe I should just let her go; none of this was any of my business, after all. But it pissed me off that she had used me and absconded with my two thousand dollars, the money that was rightfully mine and that was to finance my trip to Bucharest in June.

The more I thought about it, the more steamed I became. I had another cup of thick hot chocolate and felt my veins buzz. How on earth could I ever track Frankie down? Barcelona had literally hundreds of hotels and *hostales* and *pensiones*. Even if I had the leisure to check out each one, it would take me weeks. I was far more likely to run into Frankie in a restaurant or a bar. She struck me as a night owl. Here she was in Barcelona, after all. Was she the type to sit in some hotel room and watch Spanish television or play solitaire? I doubted it. Barcelona's night life was famous all over the world. Frankie must know that. I needed to do some serious bar-hopping tonight, and I needed some help.

Carmen ignored me when I came into the beauty salon. The receptionist said my favorite hairdresser was occupied and asked me to take a seat. But I sidled up to Carmen's workstand where she was grimly fastening rollers into the dyed black hair of a heavily made-up *señora*, and whispered:

"I know why you were so upset yesterday."

"*Sí?*" Said with brutal dismissiveness.

"At first I thought it was because Frankie was an American. . . . "

"Sí?"

"But now I know it was because she was a he."

The señora under Carmen's fingers jumped.

"Sí?" It could be such a curt word sometimes.

"I know your nephew is. . . " I paused and then skipped the word, *transvestite*. "And I know you have. . . feelings about that. But he might be able to give us the names of bars and clubs where we could find Frankie. You see, I've lost her. And it's very important that I find her."

"Aiee!" screamed the señora. "You're pulling my hair."

"Think about it, Carmen," I said. "I'll meet you at eight at that bar by the Paral.lel metro stop."

It was a lovely evening, dark and warm. I arrived at the bar on Avinguda del Paral.lel a little early, found a seat outside and ordered a Campari and soda. Across the street was the Teatro Apollo where impersonator Julio Sabala was playing. A huge sign announced all the entertainers he would mimic: Frank Sinatra, Prince, Julio Iglesias, Stevie Wonder, Michael Jackson. No women though. I drank my Campari and watched the parade of people walking by. I wasn't positive that Carmen would actually show up, so I'd also asked Ana if she wanted to come along.

I didn't know why Carmen always had to be so proper and outraged. You'd think, in a family where one sister had sex for a living and the other had sex for fun, that nobody would mind if the prostitute's son was a transvestite. But I suppose they had to draw the line somewhere. The last time I'd visited Barcelona Carmen had been in a complete tizzy about it. Pablo was only nineteen and his mother had caught him dressed up in her underwear and high heels. He'd had on one of her wigs and was putting on make-up. And he'd been so brazen. He said that he'd been doing it for five years, that he often went out at night dressed as a woman.

"What have I done wrong?" Conchita, Carmen's sister, had wailed. "How could I have raised such a son?" When Carmen had told me about it I had expressed more interest than horror, and wondered aloud why it was that women could wear clothing formerly reserved to men, while it was an incredible, and therefore incredibly exciting, taboo for men to wear women's clothing. Carmen hadn't appreciated the sublety of my argument. "Men should be men," she'd shouted. "Women should be women."

"What about you?" I said. "Are you a woman if one of the definitions of woman is only being attracted to men?"

But Carmen didn't like such bold references, just as her sister had never admitted to anyone she was a prostitute. She only had "*amigos,*" just as Carmen only had "*amigas.*"

I assumed from the way Carmen had reacted about Frankie that her feelings about Pablo hadn't changed, and that Pablo, perhaps, had been ejected from the family fold for not playing fair, that is, not sleeping at home at night.

Then I saw Carmen crossing the street towards me. She was smoking a cigarette, which she almost never did in public, and looking a bit daring with her frosted hair and zebra-printed shirt underneath a blazing red jacket. She was wearing her high high heels and a tight short red skirt.

"I'm only going with you because I'm afraid that something will happen to you by yourself," she said, sitting down at the table. "Barcelona is a dangerous city. You think it's not, Cassandra, but I tell you it's changing."

"I believe you," I said. "Is Pablo coming with us?"

"He can't tonight," she said. "He works very late at his job. He's in computers now. We're very proud of him."

"But he had some suggestions?"

"Some places. Some streets. Some bars."

Ana, in a white shirt, jeans and suit jacket with the cuffs turned up, slipped into a seat next to us. She had her long hair bundled under a fedora and was chewing gum. She looked a little like Warren Beatty in *Bonnie and Clyde.*

"*Hola mujeres,*" she kissed us both. "I'm here to keep an eye on you, Carmen." Her tone was light but Carmen took offense.

"You'd better keep an eye on Cassandra. She is a wild woman but she doesn't know it."

I got up from the table with a James Dean swagger and put my hands in my bomber jacket. "Shall we hit the streets, girls? Don't worry, you're safe with me."

Both of them snorted and grabbed my arms, bearing me off to the red-light district.

8

The first time I thought I saw Frankie in the Barri Xines was early on, when we'd barely had anything to drink and I was still trying nervously to find ways for Carmen and Ana to get beyond their language differences.

It was the hour when the *barrio* began to turn itself inside out, like an ordinary shabby cloth raincoat with a garishly dyed rabbit-fur lining. It was the hour when there was still some overlap, when a conscientious girl of twelve, dressed in a simple cotton skirt and blouse and carrying a mesh bag filled with a long loaf, a bottle of mineral water and several carefully wrapped eggs bought from the tiny corner shop, could pass on a narrow sidewalk a dumpy, beaming Filipino sailor in his best whites with his arm protectively around a lanky hooker, probably a transvestite, in shimmering red sequins and gold lamé.

The three of us were in a simple, open-to-the-street bar on Carrer la Unió, between a skimpy lingerie shop and a bridal salon. The bar was packed with olive-skinned men in dark suits, all smoking furiously and watching a soccer game on the television overhead. We stood at the long linoleum bar, which was covered with unappetizing plates of oily gray octopus and greasy yellow "salads" of peas, carrots and mayonnaise.

"It's very simple," said Carmen, flashing her gold tooth wickedly. "A Catalan word is a Castilian word cut in half."

"Catalan is an older language than Castilian, with far more of a history," Ana countered. "It comes from medieval Provençal. It's the language of courtship and poetry."

71

"It has a very harsh sound," said Carmen. "Not a pure sound at all. Not poetic or romantic."

"It has power and beauty," said Ana. "*I* know. Because I speak both languages and I have a chance to compare."

"I think we'd better switch to English," I suggested. "After all, it's fast becoming the universal language."

"Coca-Cola," said Ana in disgust. "*That's* a real contribution to world culture."

"Hello, I am very happy to meet you," Carmen said in English. "What is your name? My name is Carmen."

"My name is Ana. I am so glad to make your acquaintance. How do you like London?"

"It is very rainy here."

They were mocking me. But I guessed it was better than them mocking each other.

"Would you like a drink of something?" Ana asked Carmen.

"Thank you. I would like a Coca-Cola."

"The drink of Yankee imperialism. What a good choice."

"Thank you. I like it."

They nudged each other and laughed. I glanced out the open bar door and across the street I saw her.

She didn't have auburn curls and she didn't have a faded brown pageboy. She was platinum blond and her wig cascaded down her back.

"It's her," I said. "I recognize the shoes, the way she walks."

I grabbed their arms and Ana tossed down a thousand-peseta note. We dashed out of the bar. But the sidewalks were jostlingly full, and cars travelling slowly made it impossible to run in the street. She was a block ahead of us and I saw her turn into a side street. By the time we got there she was gone.

"She was probably just a whore," said Carmen, teetering on her high heels.

"She probably saw us," I said.

"Of course she ran," said Ana, leaning against a wall. "Wouldn't you if you saw three women tearing after you?"

We went into a nearby bar. The customers were workers in worn blue cloth jackets and we were the only women.

"*Sí señores?*" the man behind the counter said to me and Ana. Maybe Carmen was the only woman.

Ana and I each had a beer and Carmen another Coke, and Carmen described Frankie to the bartender.

"A man wearing women's clothes?" he said. "There are lots of them here in the *barrio.*"

"She's not a man anymore," I put in. "She's a woman now."

The bartender, hearing my voice, took me in. "Like you?" he said. "You were a woman and became a man?"

Up to now it had been a joke. "I'm a woman and I've always been a woman," I said sharply. "The only thing I've ever been besides a woman is little Catholic girl with pigtails."

The bartender eyed me curiously. "Oh, you're American," he said, as if that explained something.

Ana and Carmen dragged me to a table.

"You let yourself in for this, Cassandra," said Carmen. "Before you cut your hair you looked fine."

Ana settled her fedora more firmly on her head. "I'm enjoying looking like a man tonight. I feel much safer somehow in the streets. And I like the idea of playing with my male side."

"I have no desire to be a man," sniffed Carmen. "Smelly big creatures." She lit a cigarette and crossed her silky legs so her skirt rode up.

"When I was young I used to want to be a boy," I said. "Not now. Of course the perks are nice. Statues in all the public squares, legislation with your name on it, 42 seconds in the toilet instead of 76. But the *guilt.* The *shame.* And don't forget baldness."

"I don't understand it," Carmen brooded. "My nephew Pablo says he doesn't want to be a woman, he just likes to wear women's clothing. He says he finds it erotic. And so does his girlfriend."

"His girlfriend!" said Ana. "What's she like?"

"She's Catalan," said Carmen gloomily.

"I don't think people change their sex for erotic reasons," I said. "It must be something deeper, more existential. Otherwise why would you go through surgery and everything?"

"There's sexual play, and then there's necessity," said Ana. "How can we understand another's necessity?"

I looked at her. She didn't appear at all like a man to me. A woman in a fedora and a suit jacket, that was all.

"My name is Carmen," Carmen said in English. "I am woman. Please, what are you? Woman or man?"

"Neither," I said, in English, then in Spanish, "I'm a translator."

The next time I thought I saw Frankie was two or three hours later. We had been rigorously patrolling the streets and alleyways of the *barrio* with frequent stops for refreshment. We had come, at the time when the night began to grow eerier, to a sinister neighborhood of blasted streets with barricaded buildings and empty lots. A few tenements had been half demolished; high above, their rooms had a shocked, broken-in look. A few people scavenged in the lots and along Carrer de les Tàpies some older prostitutes sat on chairs outside a derelict bar and a nameless hotel.

"Look," I hissed. I grabbed Carmen's and Ana's arms, and pulled them close to a wall. Crossing in front of us was a woman with curly red hair.

"I thought you said she was blond," Ana complained.

"I must have made a mistake earlier. This has got to be her. The wig's the same, and that walk. Unmistakable."

"All prostitutes walk like that," Carmen complained.

"The wide shoulders, the narrow hips," I said. "I'm sure it's Frankie. The mini-skirt, those big feet."

We were creeping along the side of the wall. The red-haired figure had turned down a street where hookers and customers stood in the middle of the sidewalk and discussed activities and prices. She walked casually, holding her big purse at her side, and glancing around with evident interest.

"Come on," I said.

Ana giggled. "I'm drunk," she said.

"Get a grip," I told her. "You've only had a couple of beers."

Carmen took Ana's arm. "Pretend you're my man," she said. She wiggled her behind.

"I thought I was your man," I protested.

"No, you walk more quickly. Catch up with her. See if you're right."

"All right." I shot forward while trying to look inconspicuous. I hunched my shoulders together and pulled my neck down into my bomber jacket. The crowd increased. At the next corner were a police wagon and an ambulance; medics were bringing a man out from a doorway on a stretcher. His face was covered with a white cloth and he had lost a shoe. Neon lights rained down on us like blood. The gutters were choked with garbage, there was a rank sweaty smell in the air. The police told us to move along, but the crowd heaved intractably. I got pushed up against a building. A hooker said, "How about it?," then saw my eyes and backed away. At the edge of the crowd I saw Ana and Carmen looking worried. The red-haired woman was nowhere in sight.

The last time I thought I saw Frankie was much much later, at a barnlike gay bar in a residential district that was the last place we visited that night. It was so thick with smoke that it was hard to breathe, and there were two big bouncers outside the door and two inside who only let Carmen in because she was with two men.

We had heard that there was a "show" of female impersonators there, but it wasn't on that night. Instead platoons of men, working men, not the trendies of the upscale bars, danced disco and smoked and stood around.

"Most of them live with their mothers," Carmen said tenderly. "They come here to relax once or twice a week."

We had given up on finding Frankie and were in the dulled but open state of mind that comes with a late evening and too much to drink. We had another beer each and discussed all manner of things in a corner of the big smoky room. Carmen, filled with Andalucían *duende*, recited lines from Lorca poems and sang snatches of *cante jondo*, while Ana, with a somber depth of feeling, told us stories of her late mother's life in exile in France after the fall of Barcelona.

I was holding forth on the subject of translation.

"Every author has a vocabulary and once you understand that half your job is done. The last writer I translated had a very mechanical way of phrasing ideas; his book was full of pistons and levers and drills and pumps and so on. Gloria's vocabulary is romantic: heart, jungle, loin, flaming, river, lust—I could make a list of a hundred words and that would be her novel, the same words over and over."

I had a sip of beer and a potato chip. "Architecture has a vocabulary too. And hairstyling."

"Poof, frizz, tease, sculpt, trim," said Ana brightly.

"Curve, buttress, tower, skyscraper, gargoyle," said Carmen, not to be outdone.

The disco music blared loud and violent, until suddenly it shifted into the familiar notes of the Sevillana. As the three of us watched, transported, two long lines of men arranged themselves opposite each other and lifted their arms in the classic curve of that graceful, ubiquitous Spanish dance. They twisted their wrists, flourished their palms, snapped their fingers, moved forward and back and around each other, caught each other by the waist and twirled each other quickly around and around. Those who weren't dancing gathered together and clapped their hands in a regular beat.

That's when I thought I saw Frankie again. Across the smoky room, her brown hair tied back in a ponytail, dressed in a suit but looking like a man rather than a woman, I thought I saw her triangular face and bright hazel eyes, her hands lifted, clapping. But it was so cloudy in that room, so crowded, so hectic that I couldn't be sure. I thought our eyes met, I took a step towards her, and then I lost her again.

"What is it, Cassandra?" Carmen said, catching me as I stumbled. "Are you trying to dance?"

I was drunker than I should have been, or more confused. For a second I had lost the sense of who I was—what sex, what gender, what age, what city and what country. In the instant I saw the man or woman who may or may not have been Frankie I had one of those odd, powerful, and probably alcohol-induced revelations that seem to last forever and wind backwards and forwards into history and infinity.

Afterwards I could never say what it was I experienced just then. But it was as if I were at a masquerade ball and everyone, at the very same moment, lifted their masks, and I saw gender for what it was, something that stood between us and our true selves. Something that we could take off and put on at will. Something that was, strangely, like a game.

Behind me I heard Carmen and Ana conferring worriedly.

"Is she sick, is she going to be sick?"

I wanted to reassure them that I was fine, but I couldn't remember what language we'd been speaking and which one they understood.

"We'd better get her out of here," they decided and dragged me away from my epiphany, and from the person who I later decided could never have been Frankie.

The taxi dropped us off at three in the morning, at a time when the streets were still ablaze but there was little traffic and only a few people walking along the enormous boulevards. There was a message on the answering machine.

"It's for you," said Ana, and we ran it through again.

"Sorry about the misunderstanding, Cassandra," said Frankie in that cheerful, throaty voice. "I can explain everything tomorrow. Meet me at that big Gaudí cathedral around one o'clock."

9

There was not much point in going to sleep so I spent the morning taking aspirin and working on the translation, as a kind of expiation for my sins.

The plot of *La Grande y su hija* was not as complicated as one would think at first from the narrative style of dashing and drifting back and forth in time between María's own life (what she knew she had experienced) and Cristobel's life (most of it imagined by María). The plot was rather simple actually, in spite of the extraordinary number of coincidences and mysterious circumstances, starting with the disappearing plague in the first chapter. María's life began at the moment she knew her mother had vanished, but Cristobel's life had begun some twenty-five years before, and it was that life which was the primary subject of *La Grande*.

So far María had traced her mother's story back to the time when Cristobel was six and had first appeared floating down a vast river in a barrel. She was plucked to safety by the captain of a barge, who was unable to get from her the story of the barrel, but who took her home to his childless wife. The woman, Pilar, of course hated little Cristobel on sight and kept her ignorant and half-starved for years, until she finally married her off, a few weeks after the kindly barge captain disappeared into the river (I suspected his eventual reappearance), to a suspicious salesman named Raoul. But here perhaps I should let María imagine Raoul.

No one knew for sure what it was that Raoul sold from his shabby black leather bag. He kept it locked and the key on a chain next to his heart, so that when he forced himself on his young wife, which in the beginning was as often as six or eight times a day, she saw the key, shiny as the blade of a knife, dangling above her, untouchable, like a prisoner's vision of freedom.

Raoul was a travelling salesman and by rights he should have left Cristobel at home when he set off on a sales trip, but because he knew that she would bolt as soon as he took his eyes off her, he was compelled to take her with him. It was in this way that Cristobel visited every inhabited corner of her country, every river village, every mountain hamlet, every mining town, every isolated outpost on the *pampas*. And yet, even after months of following Raoul, she still did not know what it was he sold.

When they came to a village or a farmhouse, Raoul would gather the men of the place together in a room by themselves and lock the door. Outside the women of the village or ranch would stand anxiously, listening to their men laugh and snort and gasp, and they would pelt Cristobel with questions: what was in that bag, what had he come to sell, her husband?

But Cristobel did not know.

And, as a matter of fact, I did not know either, not having come to Gloria's explanation. I suspected something to do with sex, something rather nasty and small (because he could travel long distances without replenishing his bag). Aphrodisiacs or vials of something that would ensure potency.

But back to the plot, which continued with Raoul's death, perhaps at the hands of Cristobel, or perhaps Eduardo. I had come to suspect that Raoul was attached to a right-wing paramilitary organization led by former German Nazis, and that Eduardo first seduced Cristobel in order to spy on Raoul, but I wasn't sure.

María was the daughter of Eduardo and Cristobel, but the

disappearing plague had forced Cristobel to give María up as a baby. María had been raised by a kindly woman named Raquel who had told María stories about her mother and her two men. When María was seventeen Raquel died and María set off to find her mother. The narrative was both the story of her search and her imaginary reconstruction of her mother's life, which took María all over the the nameless Caribbean country in the grip of cataclysmic events. Yet Cristobel, witness to so much history and madness, was essentially passive. She spent most of her time waiting for Eduardo to turn up and when he did he would say things like, "My love, you'll never understand. Let's not talk politics," before fleeing back into the jungle.

And there were far too many passages like this:

> Theirs was a love that had existed for centuries in the genes of those who had come before, the exiled Spanish grandee first casting eyes on the Indian servant girl, reading mystery in her eyes, the mystery of a new continent. . . .

I worked until twelve-thirty when I took some more aspirin and set off to meet Frankie.

The unfinished cathedral of Sagrada Família was Gaudí's masterpiece and the building to which he'd dedicated the better part of his life; still, it always gave me an uneasy feeling. Sometimes it looked like a giant hand had been playing on the beach and had dropped wet sand, layer after layer, to form a series of towers that began lumpishly and ended in filigreed elegance. Sometimes it looked like a mud-brown excrescence worming its way out of the earth into all sorts of elongated gothic excesses. Sagrada Família was dedicated to St. Joseph and the Holy Family, and was meant to symbolize the stability and order of family life. Perhaps that was what gave me such a queasy sensation when I looked at the cathedral; it was monumentally, phenomenally bizarre, like the Christian notion of family itself, a combination of organic and tortured form.

I found Frankie at one of the main entrances, the façade of the Nativity, which was dripping with figures of angels, animals and of course the Holy Family itself. She was in white and pink today, fresh and virginal in a big candy-striped shirt over a mini-skirt, and accessorized with white sandals, a dozen bangles and the usual enormous handbag the size of a small refrigerator. She had her auburn curls back and they looked more festive than ever; her skin shone and her lipstick was a fun pink. She appeared far too healthy and well-rested to have spent the evening in the Barri Xines. Unlike me—a walking spectacle of over-indulgent remorse.

I realized that I didn't know whether to think of her as a "she" or a "he" now. She looked the same to me as she had the last time I saw her, but now that I "knew" she had been born a male, I could see that she still resembled a man in slight ways. A certain boniness around the chin, larger hands and feet, perhaps the muscularity of her legs. Still, I'd met plenty of women who were bigger, stronger, bonier and more muscular than Frankie.

In what did her masculinity reside then? Her voice was low, but I'd thought that came from smoking. She had breasts and hips and the gestures and movements of a woman. She was more feminine than I or many of my women friends. It wasn't only surgery that had changed her sex, or hormones, it was a conscious choice to embrace femaleness, whatever femaleness is.

Frankie's reaction to my hesitation was to sweep me up in a cloud of L'Air du Temps perfume and to kiss my cheek. "Don't think I'll ever forget what you've done for me, Cassandra. Leading me to my little daughter who I missed so terribly." And she held out a check for $2500. "Now don't say no to the bonus. Just something to make up for my having had to mislead you a tiny bit."

I suppressed the suspicion that by the time I deposited the check in my bank account in London it would have been cancelled or would bounce. After all, we'd never said cash. "I'd say you misled me more than a tiny bit," I said mildly. "In the first place you never mentioned a child, and in the second place 'Bernadette' is hardly your ex-husband, much less your husband."

Frankie started. "Oh, I see you've talked to Ben then?"

"I raced Hamilton to the park and found out you'd just tried to kidnap Delilah."

She ignored that. "Well, if you've talked to Ben you can understand why I think of her that way, as an ex-husband." Frankie waved her hand airily. "She's so *butch*. She's always been so much more of a man than me. How could I have told you the real story, about my baby Delilah? You'd never have come with me then."

"That's true," I admitted. "But I don't understand why you had to come to Barcelona at all. According to Ben they're just here for a vacation."

"You don't quit your job just to go on a vacation," said Frankie. "Do you? You don't sublet your apartment in San Francisco for a year, do you? You don't buy an open-ended ticket, do you?"

Frankie fixed me with an accusing look, as if I had personally arranged for Ben's flight.

"You're sure about all that?"

"Of course I'm sure. When Ben didn't bring Delilah over to my apartment Saturday morning two weeks ago I wasn't too worried. It was the kind of thing she'd done before, gone out of town suddenly without giving me the courtesy of a call. But on Monday when I called Federal Express they said she no longer worked there. Her home phone number was disconnected and no one answered the door. It took me days to find out that she'd sublet to a friend of a friend who wouldn't tell me *anything*. I called every travel agent in the Bay Area to find the agent who'd issued the tickets; when I found out it was Barcelona I got really worried. So I called the phone company and said some calls to Barcelona had been charged to my phone and could they tell me the phone number. They did, and that's when I decided I needed to come over here. And that I needed help."

"And Lucy?"

"It's true what I told you about Lucy, more or less. I ran into her on the street and told her I was thinking of going to Spain and did she know anyone who lived there. She said no, but after we'd talked awhile she mentioned you in London, and I said I'd like to give you a call when I passed through London. She says hi, by the way."

"Oh, thanks," I said.

Frankie and I began walking around the cathedral, which towered over us like a frozen dream.

"Don't be too hard on me, Cassandra," Frankie said. "I'm so alone here. It took a lot of courage to come."

In spite of myself I unbent a little. "Can't you talk to Ben about all this?"

"If I could get her alone I'd love to talk with her. But April's always with her, and I can't stand April. Not that I really know her, but she seems like one of those smug *spiritual* types who thinks having been born a woman means she has a direct link with the cosmos. As if it weren't completely *accidental* what sort of bodies we were born into. I mean, look at Ben. Ben has lots more male energy than I have! It's so ironic that just because she has a real uterus she was able to have our baby and not me!"

Frankie's voice had risen and a small group of young American tourists who had been listening to a lecture on Gaudí's "freer approach to the design of supporting structure and consequently of the building's ultimate shape," stared at us uneasily.

"It sounded to me as if the issue was also about what you did with Delilah on the weekends."

"But I'm a perfect mother," said Frankie. "I take her to the zoo and McDonalds, to the Exploratorium and Fishermen's Wharf."

"What about at night?"

"I don't judge Ben for how she earns her living. As an actress I have to be free for auditions and rehearsals. What does she expect? Just because she gave up her dreams of the theater doesn't mean I have to." She sighed. "Besides, women don't make very much money."

We walked around in silence for a while, occasionally crossing paths with the American tourists and their guide, who was praising Gaudí's "encyclopedic taste," and pointing out how Gaudí loved to show quite openly the process of construction and assembly. After many years of neglect during the Franco years, Sagrada Família was again in the process of contruction, and there were piles of stones everywhere and tall cranes beside the towers.

"So how does Hamilton fit into the picture?" I asked.

"He doesn't really. He's a friend of April's, I think from high school or something."

"I know you met him that day I followed April and Ben to the park. What did you talk about?"

Again Frankie hesitated. "I explained myself as best I could, told him what had happened, that I only wanted to see Ben and Delilah and talk to them. He said he'd discuss it with Ben and then meet me for lunch the next day."

"But instead of meeting him—and me—you went to Parc Güell and tried to kidnap Delilah."

"That's a total misconstruction of what happened. Yes, I went to the park. I admit I wanted to see my daughter. Is that a crime?" Frankie stopped and looked at me defiantly. "Is that a crime?"

"It's not a crime," I said, "but—"

"Do you have any understanding of what it is to love a child and not be able to see that child except on the weekends for a few hours? To not be able to participate in that child's life, to hear how her day at school went and what she dreams and thinks about? To know that every minute you don't spend with that child she's hearing lies and falsehoods about you—about your work, your sexuality, your very being? And then to have that child taken away from you? To have that child simply disappear and realize that you may never see her again?"

We had circled the construction site and were back in front

of the Nativity façade. The angels trumpeted above us.

"I don't know," I admitted. "I have a few nieces and nephews but—"

"Of course I said hello to Delilah," Frankie interrupted. "Isn't a parent allowed to speak to her child? And then Ben saw me and started screaming bloody murder. Of course I left. I hate scenes."

"What are you planning next?"

"I thought that maybe you could talk to Ben," Frankie said.

"Forget it. My job is over. I'm on my way back to London and then I'm going to Bucharest."

"But Cassandra, I don't have anybody else here."

"What about Hamilton?"

"Hamilton's not really a friend."

"I don't know," I shook my head. "First Ben wants me to talk to you and then you want me to talk to Ben. I think you need to talk to each other."

"April's always around. Ben won't do anything without April."

"What if I keep April occupied?" I said, with only a slight ulterior motive. "While you meet with Ben."

"Do you mean today?"

"I'll go over there this evening," I promised.

"Then I'll call Ben and arrange to meet her."

Frankie and I shook hands under the scene of the Holy Family. She had a strong grip.

10

When I called the apartment at La Pedrera later that afternoon April answered, warm and a bit breathy.

"Yes, Frankie called. They're going out for a drink in a little while."

"That's great," I said encouragingly. "I'm sure they'll work something out."

"I don't know," murmured April. "It's often hard to know what the right thing to do is."

"I'm sure it's a difficult situation for you." I was sympathetic, pretending the idea had just struck me. "Look, why don't I come over while Ben is gone? I'm right in the neighborhood. We could talk."

April appeared to hesitate.

"I'm right in the neighborhood," I repeated, and then, more daringly, "You know, I've never forgotten that foot massage you gave me. It was one of the great sensual experiences of my life."

I couldn't be any bolder than that without risking humiliation.

But April seemed to like it. "Well," she purred throatily. "I don't see why you couldn't come by. Around seven-thirty? Ben is meeting Frankie at seven. And we can talk."

The bank that now owned La Pedrera was experimenting with all-night illumination. Huge klieg lights shone onto the wavy façade. It looked like a giant seashell stranded in a pool of phosphorescence. How could anyone inside sleep at night?

The *portero* in the Provença entry was still on duty. I gave him my name and he called up to the apartment for permission to let me ascend.

"It's wonderful that my friends are able to stay in such a nice place," I volunteered. "Especially *el Señor* Kincaid. How long has he been here now? Two years, three?"

The *portero* appeared to nod.

"Funny, he doesn't seem like an American," I murmured.

"Because he's not," said the *portero*. "He's from Eastern Europe somewhere. He and his friends."

If this guy thought there were women like Ben and April in Krakow or Prague he was sadly mistaken. But why had Hamilton told him such a thing?

The *portero* held the elevator door open and I gave him a tip.

It was a short trip up to the second floor but a trip back in time. The elevator was finished in walnut, with a curved seat and an art nouveau mirror. The elevator opened into a small foyer off which there were only two doors. One of them was open.

"Cassandra," April took both my hands and drew me inside. "How good, how really *good* to see you."

I felt my blood tingle slightly. April hadn't let go of me and her hands, like those of many masseuses, were dry and strong and very much alive. She was wearing a gauzy Moroccan caftan with nothing much underneath. Not that you could see through it, but the shape of her large body was pretty clear and deliciously round and full. Her black hair was newly washed and very frizzy around her full face; it gave off a dizzying odor of soap and fragrant oils. Crystals and rose quartz hung down between her breasts.

"It's great to see you too," I said weakly. "Nice place Hamilton has here."

All the apartments in La Pedrera were arranged around two central courtyards, like an egg with a double yolk. When you came into the apartment there was a corridor making a windowed half-circle around the courtyard, and from this corridor rooms of various sizes led off; the large ones gave onto the street, and the smaller ones onto a view of roofs and courtyards. The shape of the apartment was like a pie, and we, in the living room, were at the fluted edge of the crust.

April gave me a little tour. "I don't know if you're interested in architecture, but there's lots more here than meets the eye. Many people don't realize that in addition to being a visionary, Gaudí was technically very very sound." April pointed to the wall between the living and dining rooms. "Gaudí constructed the building with pillars that bear all the weight, so the walls of the rooms can be moved and changed. And look at this stucco decoration," she pointed to the lintels around the doors and windows. "The wavy patterns are formed by fingers." I looked up. The ceilings had patterns too, but they looked as if they'd been brushed on; the patterns were the shapes of sand underwater or when the tide has receded.

"How can Hamilton afford a place like this?"

"Oh, he's subletting," April said vaguely and led me past a back door to show me the kitchen and the rather small bedrooms. "Delilah's sleeping," she said, pointing to a closed door. "She had a long day."

"Now what can I get you? Tea or a drink of something?"

"Tea's fine," I said. "Subletting from whom?"

"I'm not really sure," April said. She looked uncomfortable.

A wealthy Czech who had fled in 1968 and perhaps gone back, but wanted to keep his investment? The Czechs liked the saxophone, I knew. Hamilton could have a jazz connection.

April brewed up a pot of mysterious-smelling tea and led me back into one of the main rooms. The blinds were shut against the fierce outside illumination. Much of the interior had been decorated with Modernista furniture and rugs. "I was just studying Spanish when you came," said April, pointing to some books. "And I pulled this out for you. You might like to borrow it," she said, handing me a volume with a large foot on the cover. It was *Stories the Feet Can Tell* by Eunice D. Ingham.

She pulled me down, not onto the sofa, but onto the floor. April was one of those California types who sit cross-legged a lot. My bones creaked as I joined her, but my stiffness was easy to forget in the warmth of her gorgeous full presence. Close-up I saw she had a tiny spattering of freckles in her cleavage. It wasn't going to be easy to keep my mind on business.

In a natural and easy way, she began to remove my sandals as she asked, "Did you get any kind of explanation from Frankie about why she'd come here?"

"She was obviously worried that you and Ben were taking more than a vacation. She said she found out that Ben quit her job and that the ticket was open-ended."

With a practiced air April pulled both my naked feet up on her lap. I felt the warmth of her big soft thighs and her firm hands. "Inhale." She grasped both soles and pressed a thumb right under the ball. "Now exhale. That's your solar plexus." She pinched into the fleshy part of each of my big toes. "Your pituitary reflex... Ben was wanting to quit her job anyway. And she only had a week's vacation saved up. It's still a vacation."

"But she sublet her apartment for a year, Frankie said."

"She did?" Then she laughed. "Oh yes, I forgot. She said she wouldn't have much money when she went back to San Francisco. She was going to sublet her apartment and live with a friend to build up some savings."

That sounded pretty elaborate for a short vacation. And I noticed that April said nothing about going back to San Francisco herself. Not for the first time the thought crossed my mind that things might not be quite right between April and Ben. Along with the thought that perhaps, just perhaps, Frankie had been justified in pursuing Ben to Barcelona.

April stroked the back of my right calf up to my sole and cupped my foot with both hands. Then, holding my heel in one hand, she gently rotated the toes. She twisted her fist into the bottom of my foot, then wrung the entire foot several times.

I could feel the weight of her fingers travelling all the way up to my lower back and spine.

"Your organs all have reflex points at the bottom of your feet," she said seriously. "That's why it's called Reflexology." She'd told me that, in practically the same tone of voice, dreamy and knowing, the last time she'd massaged my feet after the march in San Francisco, but I'd forgotten it. "Your feet are the part of you furthest from the heart, so, with the natural process of gravity, impurities settle in your feet and calcify, right next to tiny nerve endings. What we're trying to do is stimulate those deposits so they break up and are carried away."

"Can you feel anything is wrong with my organs?" I asked.

She smiled at me. "This is a massage, not a diagnosis. We're just sending a little message from your feet to those organs: if there is anything wrong then they need to get a move on healing themselves. We're just opening up the pathways."

The wires must be crossed though, because the main message that was getting through was going directly to a place between my legs.

I tried to keep my mind on the subject of Frankie. "The sense I got from Frankie was that she wouldn't have bothered to fly to Barcelona to see Delilah if she hadn't been frantic with worry about losing her. She really loves the kid and wants her in her life."

"It's so hard to know what's right," April murmured. "In the best of all possible worlds, every child would have parents who loved and nurtured her and/or him."

"It sounds to me like Delilah does have two parents," I said. "And you too, of course." I wondered if there was some rivalry between April and Frankie, if that was the reason April had persuaded Ben to bring Delilah to Barcelona.

April didn't respond to that; in fact she seemed hardly to have heard what I said. She had a firm hold of my right foot and was grinding her thumb gently into my organs, I mean my reflex points, with controlled abandon. "Just breathe naturally," she said, with a seductive look under her violet lids. "You sound a little congested. I'll work a little on your bronchial tubes."

It's true that my breath was coming in little gasps, but it wasn't from blocked bronchial tubes. "Don't stop," I said. "That one place you were just touching. . . it was very good. . . the way you were touching it. . . . "

91

"Here?" she inquired in a low voice, and fit the heel of my foot more firmly into her lap as she pressed out those pesky little calcifications from the ball of my foot in steady, rhythmic movements. I moaned aloud.

"That's good," April said, "Don't keep it inside, let your voice out."

I moaned again. Louder. And again.

The feet are highly underrated, I thought.

"Hi everybody!" said Hamilton, coming into the room. We hadn't heard him open the front door.

"Hi," said April, shifting my foot unobtrusively from her lap. Her cheeks were slightly flushed. "Cassandra came by to talk about Frankie. I was just giving her a foot massage." April slapped my foot with brisk professionalism.

"That's right," I said. "My organs have gotten a message and I think it's a good one."

Hamilton stood there in his blue leather ostrich boots and looked at me without any particular friendliness. I had the sense that he hadn't forgiven me for pretending to be Brigid yesterday.

"Do you want some tea, Hamilton?" April said, a little nervously.

He didn't answer her. "Where's Delilah? Is she all right?"

"Of course," April said. "I put her to sleep after Ben left, around seven. She was exhausted, poor thing."

"I'll just check in on her," Hamilton said.

April sighed, and when he'd left, she whispered, "He's hopelessly in love with Delilah, you know. It's bringing out all his paternal instincts."

"Just who is he, anyway?" I started to ask, but then Hamilton was back. He sank into a leather chair slung low to the ground. His blue eyes regarded me suspiciously.

"What line of work are you in, Cassandra? Unless you really are a journalist."

I didn't think Hamilton was naturally aggressive, but he

lacked humor and those without humor never appreciate having jokes played on them.

"I'm a translator. As a matter of fact I'm in the process of translating *La Grande y su hija*. Gregory Rabassa was too busy, so they thought of me."

In spite of himself he was impressed. "That's quite a coup, isn't it, Cassandra?"

"To tell you the truth, at this point I think I prefer nonfiction."

He nodded. "But surely fiction must be more demanding," he said. "I mean, non-fiction tells us about the world we live in, but fiction gives us our dreams and visions."

"Some fiction perhaps. Some, Hamilton, does not. To be blunt."

"I have to say that I was totally engrossed by *La Grande y su hija*. I thought there were echoes of García Márquez and Allende, as well as Valenzuela and Donoso, but that de los Angeles had forged her own unique style. If anyone she reminds me a little of Nélida Piñon, the Brazilian. The same sort of fabulist, the same sort of prodigious imagination."

"Hamilton has a Ph.D. in Spanish and Latin American studies from Columbia," April said, a little hardness coming into her inky black eyes. I wondered if she was warning me not to make fun of him.

"Where did you study, Cassandra?" Hamilton asked.

"Oh, I've picked up a little here, a little there."

"But where did you get your degree?"

"*La experiencia es la escuela de la vida.* Or you might say I studied intensively at the School of Hard Knocks."

"I never did anything with my degrees." Hamilton seemed sad. "I would have rather just played music, but my parents. . . . "

This time there was no mistaking the warning light in April's eyes. Only this time it was directed at Hamilton. Why?

But all she said was, "What's this *Grande* novel about, Cassandra?"

"You mean the plot?" I said. "Do you have two hours?"

Hamilton laughed. Perhaps there was a little hope for him after all. "It's really complicated, April, it can't be summed up easily." But he tried to give her some of the highlights: jungle, love, river, revolution, motherhood. Then Hamilton turned to me. "I saw *La Grande* as a political allegory as well as the riveting search for one's past. I understand that feminists have really responded to it."

"They have," I said gloomily. "I believe they see the obsessive search of María for her mother as a paradigm of the condition of contemporary woman."

"Oh, that's probably true, Cassandra, I hadn't thought of that." He sat back in his chair and gave me a look of respect.

But I was running out of literary clichés, so it was a relief when the front door opened with an unmistakable thump and muscular Ben in Levis, black boots and a motorcycle jacket marched into the living room and threw herself onto one of the gorgeously upholstered settees.

"Well, Frankie didn't show," she said. "I don't know if I'm surprised or not."

"What!" I said. "She was so eager to talk to you."

"You don't know Frankie as well as I do," Ben said. She ran her thick fingers through her brush cut so that it stood up angrily. "That's the whole history of my relationship with Frankie. I wait. She doesn't show. That's why this joint custody thing didn't work and will never work."

"Maybe something came up," I said.

"The only person she knows in Barcelona is you, so how could anything come up?"

"Did you call her?"

"I don't know where she's staying."

With a start I realized I didn't either. I'd forgotten to ask once again.

Ben eyed me suspiciously. "Just what did you talk about today?"

"Oh, I don't know, the usual. Gender. Motherhood. Architecture. Surely you're not accusing me of being the reason Frankie didn't show up?"

"All I know," Hamilton jumped in, forgetting the respectful gaze of a few moments back, "is that there's something odd about you being involved in all this."

I was stung. "I'm an innocent bystander, what do you mean? I could be at home translating an important work of South American literature."

"You've accepted money from Frankie," Hamilton said.

"She offered to pay me to find her husband, who then became her ex-husband, who then became her ex-wife. I found Ben, why shouldn't I be paid? I'm only still involved out of the goodness of my heart." And feet.

"What about you?" I counterattacked. "You've met with Frankie on your own. What did *you* talk about? And why does the *portero* downstairs think you're all Bulgarians and Hungarians? And where's your saxophone anyway, Hamilton?"

There was a pause and I saw Hamilton and April look at each other. At that moment, from somewhere in the apartment, came the sound of a door closing.

11

It wasn't the front door, by the elevator, but the back door, by Delilah's room.

"Delilah," Ben shouted and rushed down the corridor with all of us following.

But Delilah lay in a deep sleep in her little bed, defenseless in pajamas and still clutching her stuffed rabbit.

On the floor next to her, however, was a silver lighter that all of us recognized.

"He's been here, he's tried to get her again," Ben said, and dashed for the back door.

It led to the staircase I'd huffed up with the other tourists a few days earlier.

"I'll go down to the street," April said. "You can check the roof." She obviously was no more fond of climbing steps than I was, even in an emergency.

Hamilton hesitated. "I'll go with you, April."

Ben and I were already rushing up the staircase to the roof, but I still had time to wonder which one of the two didn't trust the other.

Ben's muscular legs took her up two steps at a time. Even so, I wasn't disgracefully far behind her, though my lungs complained violently, when we pelted through the arched corridor of attic space and up to the roof.

It was spectacular and I wished I had time to really look at it. The sculpted chimneys and airshafts formed even more fantastic shapes under the gauzy night sky. There was a slender moon, its light fragmented behind frequent clouds.

"I see someone," whispered Ben.

I saw nothing. The roof was less like the top of a building than a landscape of dream figures, shifting and dancing. The klieg lights didn't reach into the corners; the illumination from the street served only to make the shadows of the chimneys and vents darker and more twisted.

"You go left, I'll go right," Ben directed with a hand wave.

Back in Michigan when I was growing up we used to play a game called "Ditchum" in the humid, mosquito-laden summer nights down by the lake. It was a more tortuous form of Hide 'n Seek, in which you ran for blocks and stayed put for hours. There wasn't just one person looking for you, but a whole team of children, methodically combing the backyards, the woodpiles, the garages, the undersides of docks. I had been better at hiding than at seeking. Midway through the hunt I'd get bored, go off and look at the moon, sit on a bench and wonder how many days it would take to fly to outer space. Eventually one of my teammates or even one of the hidden children would find me sitting there. "Cathie! [I was Catherine Frances Reilly then.] You're *supposed* to be *looking.*"

I crept stealthily up and down the broad shallow steps that undulated over the roof. There were lots of places to hide here, behind chimneys, in corners... Was that a movement? No.

I couldn't even see Ben; she was over on the far side, around the second courtyard.

I prowled further. What was it about Hamilton that bothered me? There had been absolutely no musical equipment in the apartment at all. Not even a boom box. How did April know him? Why had she been so evasive about him?

Out from behind one of the chimneys a figure stepped slowly and softly. She was wearing a big sweater and she had curly hair. Frankie. I paused with my heart in my throat. If she didn't see me, if she came this way—I desperately tried to remember some karate moves. At least I could trip her, I could sit on her. . . .

She saw me and vanished again. Hell. I stopped prowling and rushed headlong after her. Rounding a corner at top speed I careened into Ben, who was also running. We knocked each other over in a good imitation of a Keystone Cops routine. But she was younger and more resilient.

"I saw her. Did you see her?" She stood up and pointed in the direction I'd come.

I nodded weakly, still winded.

Ben took off in that direction, while I contemplated my adventurous life and the moon. There was nothing like a nighttime run for getting the blood going.

From somewhere to the right I heard the sounds of a struggle, and shouting.

"Where do you think you're going?" That was Ben.

"Get your hands off me!"

"Not till you tell me what you were doing in our apartment with Delilah."

Grunts and groans.

I approached cautiously.

Ben had Frankie in a modified half Nelson. I guessed you got pretty strong working for Federal Express. All those packages.

"Cassandra, over here," Ben said.

But just at that moment Frankie broke away and dashed in the direction of the stairs.

"Never mind," said Ben. "Hamilton and April will be waiting for him."

But when we got down to the foyer there was no sign of any of them. The *portero* had gone off duty and the small door at the side of the iron gate was wide open.

"If they let him get away. . . " Ben muttered.

We went through the door and out onto the brightly lit street. Behind us La Pedrera reared up on its elephantine pillars.

I'd forgotten how early it was, probably only about nine o'clock in the evening. The streets were crowded and traffic poured up and down the Passeig de Gràcia.

"Maybe they're all having an espresso in the bar," I said.

"Maybe they're over at the music store buying saxophone tapes."

Ben glared at me. "This isn't funny, Cassandra."

We wandered around the street for a little bit and looked in the windows of the bar. Finally we saw April crossing the street toward us. She looked worried.

"Where's Frankie? Is Hamilton chasing him?" Ben demanded.

"I think so," said April. "We were each supposed to be at one of the doors. I was standing at the main door and nothing was happening, so I went over to the Provença door, but Hamilton wasn't there anymore. I guess Frankie came out that way and Hamilton went after her. She wasn't up on the roof?"

"He was," Ben said. "But he got away."

We saw Hamilton coming around the corner of Provença.

"Didn't you catch him?" Ben demanded.

"Catch Frankie? I was looking for April. She wasn't at the main door when I went to look."

"I was too," said April indignantly. "You were the one who was gone. I thought you'd gone after Frankie."

Their Keystone Cop routine was as bad as mine and Ben's had been on the roof.

"Well, the important thing," I said, to quiet their animosity, "is that Delilah's safe."

All of them looked at each other, then Ben rushed back in the door with Hamilton and April close behind her. I followed more slowly. This stampeding around was not good for my heart, I was convinced.

When I got back to the apartment by way of the back stairs I found them all shouting at each other.

Delilah, it appeared, was no longer asleep in bed.

A confused ten minutes followed. There was a great deal of shouting, name-calling and general accusation and recrimination.

Why hadn't someone stayed in the apartment?

Why didn't you stay at your door?

Why didn't *you*?

How had Frankie gotten away from Ben up on the roof?

How had Frankie gotten in to La Pedrera in the first place?

What was Cassandra's role in all this?

At which point I decided I'd had enough.

"I'm going home," I announced. "There's a good TV program on the EEC monetary policy that I'm just dying to see."

"No!" Ben panicked. "You're our only link with him. Where would Frankie have taken Delilah?"

"I don't know," I said. "The airport?"

The three of them had been so busy accusing and defending that they hadn't gotten any further.

"The airport?" Ben was aghast. "Did he tell you he planned to take Delilah back to California?"

"Of course not," I said. "Frankie never told me the truth about anything if she could help it. But it's one possibility. Why would Frankie want to keep Delilah hidden in Barcelona?"

Ben was the kind of woman who moved quickly. They must miss her at Federal Express. She grabbed my arm and started towards the back door again. "Oh god, I hope we're not too late."

"I'll stay here," April said. "In case Frankie calls or something."

Hamilton looked at her strangely. "I'll stay too," he said. "You don't need us at the airport if you have Cassandra to translate."

What was going on between April and Hamilton?

But Ben had me halfway down the stairs before I could protest. I barely had time to grab my leather briefcase with Gloria de los Angeles's prodigiously imagined opus.

In the taxi Ben clenched and unclenched her fists as we sped recklessly through the brilliant arterials of the city. At first all she could say was, "I'll kill him," but clearly she had other feelings, other doubts.

"I'm not a bad mother," she said.

"No one said you were."

"I had to get away from Frankie. Maybe I should have moved someplace like Eugene or Portland, someplace that would have been close, but that would have put an end to those weekends with Delilah."

"Barcelona is a little extreme."

"How was I to know he'd follow us here? How was I to know he'd have the... guts to take Delilah?" Ben clenched her hands and bent her head. The taxi threw her heavily against the door, and me heavily against her.

"*Cuidado*," I advised the driver, pulling away from Ben and righting myself. Her scent was a combination of fresh leather and sour sweat.

"Why did you choose Barcelona?" I said.

"April had a friend here. Hamilton's an old friend of hers."

"He makes his living as a musician, isn't that right?"

"I'm not sure if he makes his living that way," Ben said. "He's got money, family money." She added, half in pride, half in envy, "April does too."

"April?" Hamilton I could figure for a rich boy, but April?

"Well, she gets money from somewhere," Ben amended. "Some bank sends her money."

What I couldn't give to know a bank that would send me money too.

"April's a very... spiritual woman," I said.

"Yeah," sighed Ben. "The first time I met her, something just melted inside me. Those big dark eyes, those hands—god, those hands."

We reminisced separately for a moment and a desperate tone came into Ben's voice.

"I love April so much. I just feel I couldn't live without her. I met her at the New Age Bodywork Center when I went there for a pulled muscle in my leg. From the moment I saw her I knew she was the one for me." Ben's voice grew soft. "At first she wasn't particularly interested, but I pursued her. I sent her flowers, I wrote her notes, I found out her phone number and called her. I courted her. Finally she gave in."

I remembered the ambivalence in April's tone when she talked about Ben. Perhaps April hadn't given in all the way.

"She must love you a lot to have followed you to Barcelona."

Ben stared at me as the taxi screamed to a halt in front of the airport. "Yes," she said fiercely as she threw herself out of the cab. "She really loves me."

The driver accepted my tip with thanks. "I guess he's in a hurry, isn't he, *señora?*"

"Yes," I nodded. I was back to womanhood, but only because the world thinks in dyads and Ben was more of a man than me.

I found her at the departure board. "There was a flight to New York at nine, but he couldn't have gotten here in time. And there's nothing more to the States tonight."

Now that we were out of the taxi my mind cleared and a dozen other possibilities presented themselves to me. There was no reason for Frankie to have flown immediately back to San Francisco. She could have flown or be about to fly anywhere; there were flights listed to Rome, to Athens, to London and to Paris. There was even a possibility that she wasn't flying, but taking a train or a bus out of the country or even to another part of Spain.

Some of these possibilities were occurring to Ben herself. After twenty minutes of stalking nervously around the airport, scouring the restrooms and the waiting room, she subsided into a muscular slump of black leather and despair in a molded chair.

"I'm not a bad mother," she said. "I haven't neglected Delilah. Not really. I don't deserve this."

It sounded as if she were more concerned with being thought neglectful than with actually worrying about Delilah.

"If Delilah's with Frankie," I tried to reassure her, "she's probably not in any real danger. I'm sure Frankie will be contacting you."

"You don't know Frankie. He's completely unreliable. He

could be anywhere with my daughter right now." She suddenly stood up and pulled me up with her. "Why did we come to the airport? They're probably at the train station. That's where we should have gone."

So far I'd mainly seen Ben in motion, stomping about and flinging herself from place to place, but back in another taxi she grew contemplative, staring out at the bright lights of a city she hardly knew.

"Sometimes I think of my own childhood and how I grew up and my parents and everything and how I could ever explain any of this to them," she said as we travelled back through the outskirts of Barcelona. "I mean, my parents went to college, but it was an agricultural college. I grew up on the farm until they just couldn't make it anymore. If we hadn't moved to the city I would probably still be in Iowa, running the farm. Going to Cedar Rapids changed my life—I know it doesn't seem like a big place to you. . . . "

"It *is* smaller than Kalamazoo."

". . . but there were movies and shopping centers and a university with a drama department."

"So you really wanted to be in theater?"

"Both of us did, but Frankie more than me. I was into set construction." Ben stared at her hands. "It's funny thinking back, but one of the things I liked best about Frankie in those days was his imagination. He was the person who taught me that you didn't have to live the life your parents had planned for you, that you didn't have to be who they expected, that you could change. . . . "

She paused uncomfortably.

"I guess you feel that Frankie changed too much."

Ben didn't say anything for a minute. "Maybe it's hypocritical. Maybe it's hypocritical for me to say that I like to wear jeans and a crew cut and have biceps and that being mistaken for a man and called sir doesn't bother me. But I don't want to *be* a man. I'm a woman. And a mother."

"Did you ever think that there's no middle ground for men? They can't wake up in the morning and say, Oh I feel kind of like wearing my red satin dress and three inch pumps today."

"Transsexualism isn't about a middle ground. Transsexuals think they're born into the wrong body. They don't want the world to change, they just want to change their bodies."

"Why do you hate her so much?"

"I don't *hate* Frankie," Ben muttered. We were drawing near to Estació de Sants, the main train station. "I mean, maybe I do hate Frankie. But not for the reasons you think."

"It is because you're jealous?"

She looked grim about the mouth, but also as if she could almost weep. "You don't understand," she said. "Nobody understands. I didn't lose a husband or a father when Frankie did what he did. I lost, I lost. . . I lost a pal."

The taxi stopped and this time I restrained Ben from jumping out. "You're paying," I said.

We stood in the cavernous station, ten times more bustling and confusing than the airport, and now Ben did begin to weep.

"Come on, come on," I said. "A big strong girl like you, come on, come on." I led her to a bar and asked for cognacs and coffee for us both.

"I don't drink," she said. "I don't do caffeine either."

"Oh for godssakes," I said. "This isn't California." Nevertheless I ordered her a mineral water.

"Look," I said. "It's late, it's very late. We can hang around here all night in the hope that Frankie will turn up with Delilah and that somehow, somehow in all this mass of humanity we'll be able to spot them. If they haven't been through here already and left on a train to Timbuktu. If Frankie is even planning to take Delilah out of the country. Or we can go home sensibly and wait to hear from Frankie."

"You've never been a mother," she said. "You can't know how it feels."

"And I thank god for it every day," I said.

"I want to trust you, Cassandra," she said. "But I can't. I don't know how you're involved in all this."

That stung me. "You'd better ask yourself how April and Hamilton are involved."

"April? Hamilton?"

"One of them let Frankie escape."

"That's not true!"

I drank my cognac down to the bottom, and maintained a stubborn silence.

"You're just trying to alienate me from April, Cassandra. Don't think I haven't noticed you've had your eye on her. I'm not the jealous type, thank goodness, but if I thought you were trying to steal my girlfriend, I'd have to do something about it."

"You're paranoid," I said, all too aware of her well-developed forearms.

Ben put down her glass of mineral water and started to walk away. "I keep forgetting Frankie *paid* you to find me."

I took out Frankie's check from my bag and deliberately wadded it up. I'd never be able to cash it anyway.

"And now," I said. "I really am going home to sleep."

12

Who would she be [María wondered], this woman in whose womb I had been conceived, through whose loins I had passed into the light of day? Since the disappearing plague I had been looking for this mysterious woman, searching the faces of every female that I passed in the street, imagining in every touch of womanly hands the hands of my mother. I had given Cristobel supernatural powers, a face like Rita Hayworth and a body with a scent like that of a warm, fragrant loaf of bread.

And I imagined that my mother thought of me as well, saying to herself as she passed children in the street, "Now she is six, now she is eight, now she is bleeding, now she is in love, now she is married, now she has children of her own."

My story is two stories, that of my own life and that of my mother Cristobel, whom many times I am sure I have invented. I made her large because I am small, I made her Eduardo's lover because I have no lover, strong where I am weak, wise where I am foolish. She abandoned me and I could not find her, though over and over I discovered her traces. I imagined that she was searching for me too, but whenever I arrived at the place where she had been, she was gone. Sometimes there were fragments, remnants, signs: a scent of jasmine, a faded orchid, a stone dropped from a ring. There were tales of her youth, her loves, her illnesses and her triumphs. But they were told by people who also had not known her, who had, like me, only heard of her, and who had forgotten most of the story.

I was getting near the end of *La Grande* and Gloria was beginning to wind things up. Raoul had turned out to be a Nazi sympathizer and Eduardo had died in Cristobel's arms after a desperate guerilla action. María was closing in on her mother's whereabouts. But still no one knew what had been in Raoul's black bag.

It was the morning after my escapades with the Ben and Frankie family and I was deep into Gloria's romance when Ana came in with a cup of freshly steamed *café con leche* for me and sat down on the bed beside my desk.

She was wearing her usual white shirt and blue jeans and her hair was neatly braided down the back.

"You came in earlier than usual last night," she said. "Carmen teasing you again?"

"Carmen never does anything else," I said. "No, I was with my Americans. A podiatric encounter with the gypsy April, then a little quick sightseeing on the roof of La Pedrera, enlivened by wrestling displays, and then a madcap dash first to the airport and then to the train station where I heard another version of the classic story of American loss of innocence. First, the abandonment of the farm, then the corruptions of the big city, leading to the blurring of gender roles. Once you get away from the soil, basically, you're in trouble."

"What?"

I explained in more detail.

"Well of course Ben is worried. Losing her little girl like that."

"At least we know that Frankie has her."

Ana shook her head. "How did you get involved with these people? That is, *more* involved?"

"I can't help it," I said. "I keep feeling responsible in different ways. First I found out where Ben and April and Delilah were staying for Frankie, then I almost got Delilah snatched at the Parc Güell because I'd told Frankie they'd be there, and finally I was getting a foot massage from April when Frankie first got in to kidnap Delilah."

"It must have been a pretty heavy foot massage," said Ana.

"It was," I sighed. "It obviously interfered with my hearing."

Ana was thoughtful. "Have you figured out how Frankie got into the apartment?"

"There are two doors, front and back. One or both could have been unlocked. April could have done it, or Hamilton. Or they could have given Frankie a key. Or—Hamilton and Frankie could have come in together. He just appeared in the living room—and started going on about Gloria de los Angeles, probably to distract me. Or—I forgot about this—when he came in he went immediately to Delilah's room. He could have unlocked the door then."

"Why would Hamilton want to help Frankie steal Delilah? Money?"

"That's what I can't figure. Ben said he's wealthy. She said April gets checks from a bank too."

"Rich people are mysterious," said Ana. "Some of the people I deal with are swimming in money, but they're always trying to cheat me. They're truly convinced they're poor."

"Well, I suspect Hamilton," I said. "Because he doesn't have a sense of humor."

I helped Ana get ready to move the birth mother house out of the apartment to its destination in a suburb outside Barcelona. It would be a sad relief to see it go tomorrow. "I think I'll feel more like myself then," Ana said somewhat dejectedly.

"Anybody can have babies," I said to cheer her up. "Only some of us can create art. Besides, babies grow up, that's the problem. You never hear anyone say, 'Oh I really want to have a teenage dope fiend who plays loud music and brings disgusting adolescents home and thinks I'm stupid.' But that's what most people get."

"But first you get the nice part," said Ana, starting to laugh. "And anyway, my child wouldn't be a rebel."

"That's what my mother said," I remembered. "She still can't believe what happened to her baby girl."

◆

I hadn't seen Carmen since our night out. I gave her a call and asked her if she'd like to hear some jazz later on. According to Ben, Hamilton played with a Catalan trio three nights a week at a certain jazz club in the Barri Gòtic. I thought we might check it out.

There was no point in getting there early, and early in Spain means anytime before midnight. So Carmen and I had a long romantic dinner and then made a few stops at various bars along the winding streets of the Barri Gòtic before we turned up at the high-tech club that had replaced the smoky cellar I remembered. It was cool and avant-garde, with uncomfortable chairs and blotchy abstract paintings on the walls, and a hip young waiter with skinny shoulders and a shock of bleached hair like Andy Warhol's. Carmen and I were slightly out of place among the young women and men in their black turtlenecks and oversize jackets. Carmen had gotten herself up in a low-cut dress that showed a daring amount of bosom and I accompanied her as Katherine Hepburn in belted gabardine slacks and a raw silk shirt. We found seats and ordered champagne. Carmen smoked and looked around suspiciously.

"Is this a funeral? Why are all these people in black?"

"They're Catalans," I said.

"*Claro.*"

"They're *modernos.*"

"Mmm," she said, obviously aware that her cleavage was being eyed. She adjusted her spaghetti straps. "The only time I will wear black is when you die, *querida.*"

"Carmen, I'm touched."

The jazz that had been playing on the sound system tapered off and three men came forward to the performer's area. An alto sax, a clarinet and a piano. On sax was Hamilton, who stared at me for a second before smiling. I waved cheerfully.

Nobody ever said he wasn't a handsome guy. *I* wouldn't want a receding hairline and a pot belly, but I wouldn't mind having his straight nose and well-modelled lips. He was wearing jeans and an open-necked white shirt, rolled up at the sleeves, and a gold chain around his neck.

They played. And I was surprised at how good Hamilton was, how he could really sing with that sax. It wasn't fair—to have a trust fund and talent too.

Hamilton came over during the break. He told us we both looked lovely and Carmen beamed at him, even though he was speaking English.

"I heard you didn't have much luck with Ben at the airport," he said to me.

"That's right. We began to have our doubts that Frankie had even taken Delilah there."

"That occurred to April right after you left," said Hamilton. "There's no way Frankie could have gotten Delilah out of the country."

"Why not?"

"Delilah is listed on Ben's passport, not on Frankie's. Delilah doesn't have a passport of her own. She'd never have made it through passport control. Ben hadn't thought of that either. That must mean Frankie has Delilah somewhere in Barcelona."

"Why didn't you come to the airport to tell us?"

"We thought that if Frankie were somewhere in the building it would be good if we waited her out." Hamilton sipped the beer the waiter had brought him. I'd noticed that he and the bleached blond had touched hands briefly. "And, if you want the truth, I didn't want to leave April alone."

More likely she didn't want to leave you alone, I thought. "Why not?"

"I think it's possible that April might have had something to do with Delilah's kidnapping."

"But she's Delilah's co-parent now. Why would April want to help Frankie?"

Hamilton shook his head. "That I don't know yet. But Ben and April and Delilah have been living with me for two weeks now and I've had a chance to notice some things. April almost never talks directly to Delilah anymore and she doesn't seem that happy to be with either of them. I don't think she likes kids that much, and Delilah can feel it."

"It's probably just a stressful time," I said. "Neither Ben or April is working, Delilah's not in school, of course there's some tension."

"I know all that," said Hamilton patiently. "But that doesn't mean I can't still wonder if April might have had some reason for wanting Delilah out of the way."

"April's not that kind of person," I said categorically. "She's warm, loving, very friendly. . . . "

Hamilton watched my face. "I'm curious as to why neither of you heard Frankie in the apartment."

"There was nothing to hear until the door closed."

"How long were you there?"

He obviously thought *he* was interrogating *me*.

"Look, if you think I had anything to do with this, you're mistaken. Frankie hired me in London to help her locate someone who she said was her husband Ben. She later told me that Ben was her ex-husband. She never told me that Ben was a woman, that Frankie herself was a transsexual or that the two of them had a long-standing custody dispute over Delilah."

"But Frankie had hired you, right? And presumably, if she had offered you more money to help her get Delilah back, you would have accepted. You say you met Frankie earlier that afternoon at Sagrada Família. It would have been the easiest thing in the world for you to watch the building, see me and Ben come out, keep April occupied, and make sure the door was unlocked."

I was deeply offended. "I'm a Spanish translator," I said. "Not a hired kidnapper."

"Relax," said Hamilton. "I don't really suspect you. You had the opportunity, but not the motive. Unless you consider money a motive, which I don't."

Oh, rich men. They live in a world of their own.

He went on, "It's April I suspect. I don't know when or why she got in touch with Frankie, but I'd like to find out."

"I'm curious," I said. "Why is it that Ben refers to Frankie as he and you call her her?"

"I call people what they want to be called," said Hamilton. "And if Ben weren't so stubborn she would too."

"What do you think of Frankie?"

Hamilton sighed. "You have to like her. That doesn't mean you have to trust her."

The bleached blond waiter was back, asking Hamilton if he wanted anything else. With a smile that transformed his face Hamilton said, "Only you, *chico*." Then he shook my hand and said, "I'll keep in touch," and went back up to the stage.

Carmen had wandered off and was talking to the bartender. As it turned out he was also from Andalucía and they were exchanging derogatory remarks about the Catalans. I brought her back to the table and showed her the book that April had loaned me on Reflexology, *Stories the Feet Can Tell*.

"Carmen," I whispered, "Wouldn't you like a foot massage? Standing all day in high heels your feet must get awfully tired."

I pointed out some of the diagrams. "Look, from this chart you can see where the stomach is, and the thyroid, the lungs, the heart, everything. And by touching the soles of the feet you can heal things that are wrong with you." I translated, "See, you just press this point and you deal with Shoulder Trouble and Salivation Problems. Over here you've got Toxemia, Stress, Edema, Kidney Troubles, and just below your right big toe, Weight Problems, Anxiety and Thinning Hair."

"Thinning hair?" she grabbed the book. "That's a good one for me to know. Where?"

"Come back with me to Ana's and I'll show you," I said, pulling the book away. "It's better to demonstrate in person."

She allowed me to lead her out of the club onto the street and we began to walk back through the quarter to the Ramblas with our arms linked amorously in the way that is allowed to women together in Spain. Then she turned to me. "Cassandra," she said. "I would love to go home with you. But not tonight. My mother is waiting up for me."

I pressed her into a dark doorway. I hadn't really expected

anything else. Carmen kissed me passionately and moaned. She kneed me gently in the crotch. What a tease. "Carmen, Carmen, *querida*. . . "

"No, Cassandra." She was firm but gentle. "*No es posible.*"

We walked on. A small thief darted out of the shadows and tried to make off with Carmen's bag, but she gave him a good belt with the back of her hand and screeched some vengeful Andalucían curse about knives and tender parts of the male anatomy.

The port end of the Ramblas is where the tarot readers congregate, each with their own small table, sheltered candle and sign promising a future told through palms and cards.

Swarthy young gypsy women called out to us as we walked by, "Come here and let me tell your fortune." Carmen ignored them, but I was suddenly curious.

I sat down at one of the little tables and a woman with glittering eyes and a turban grabbed my hand and stared at it.

"Success but no money, travel, a lot of travel, adventure. Watch out for a woman with black hair."

"Who is it?" I said. "Can you see her more clearly?"

Carmen was shaking her head.

"Is she fat? Is her hair curly?"

"She is outside, she is naked."

"Who is this, Cassandra?" Carmen demanded.

"She is very very fat." The gypsy peered closer. "I see birds. Parrots."

"Oh god," I said.

"She is in a jungle. Yes. Naked in a jungle. With parrots. Watch out."

I saw Carmen into her taxi, then began to make my way back to the jazz club. It was late, there wasn't any point in talking to Hamilton again, and in fact I didn't want to talk to him. I wanted to see where he went after the show.

I had short hair and my bomber jacket. I had been mistaken for a man too many times to count in the past few days. There was no reason I should feel afraid. But as I left the Ramblas for the dark twisting streets of the lower Barri Gòtic, I had a feeling that someone was following me.

Was it just the echo of my feet? Several times I turned around and saw no one; other times there was a couple, or a crowd. I walked more quickly, tried to stay on the better lighted streets.

No, I wasn't imagining it. I was being stalked. A man in black, his face invisible under a hat pulled down low, and a bulging sack hanging ominously from his shoulder, was pursuing me. I heard his threatening breath, the soft pad of his leather shoes on the cobblestones. "Wait," he said in garbled Castilian.

I ran like the devil, and turned into the street where the jazz club was located just in time to see Hamilton mount a *moto* behind our bleached blond waiter and speed off without looking in my direction.

I hadn't really thought it was Hamilton following me, had I? A crowd of laughing *modernos* gushed out of the club and I attached myself to them until I came to a street where I could hail a cab.

I'd lost my pursuer. But I'd also lost my chance to see where Hamilton was going.

The phone rang, far too early the next morning. I stumbled from the guest room through a corridor filled with junk and antiques, cursing Ana's mania for collecting, and grabbed the receiver.

"Cassandra," wailed a familiar contralto voice. "They've stolen my child."

13

The hotel where Frankie had been holed up was in the Barri Xines, not far from the Palau Güell, the town house that Gaudí had built for his favorite patron at a time when the area had been up and coming instead of down and out. Squashed between seedy buildings with store fronts displaying objects both useful and risqué, the palace retained its mystery. Gaudí's architectural marvel opened up inside with rooms that made you feel as if you were in a huge medieval castle. High ceilings fretted with painted wood, long halls that fooled the eye with their grand perspectives, lovely arched windows that gave, most surprisingly, onto dreary streets and tenements instead of wooded estates or fog-shrouded lakes.

I remembered a story Ana had told me once in her detached, slightly ironic way: One day she'd gone to a reception in the Palau Güell. The reception had been to honor some well-known architect, and they had all been standing around with drinks in their hands chatting in the formal and restrained way of such receptions when someone had happened to notice that across the street was a brightly lit room in which you could see a band of pickpockets spreading watches, gold chains, rings and wallets out on the lumpy bed. Slowly the architects had drifted over to the window until the whole group was there, silently and with great fascination watching the thieves sort through their spoils.

Frankie's hotel, the no-star Hotel Palacio, wasn't the worst I'd ever been in—that honor went to a dive in Calcutta and the less said about that the better—but it probably wasn't where

Ben would have liked to imagine Delilah staying. A dirty wooden staircase led up to a small lobby on the second floor, where a pair of pinched sisters glared at me before pointing the way down the dimly lit hall to Frankie's room.

Frankie was waiting for me, dressed in tights and a sporty royal blue sweater but still somehow managing to suggest a Tennessee Williams heroine in an advanced state of dishabille. She was chainsmoking and her nails were broken and bitten. She began to cry when she saw me.

"You're the only one who can help me," she sobbed, throwing herself on the sagging bed over which hung a portrait of the Virgin in blue.

"Before we get into the matter of helping we need to sort a few things out, Frankie."

"I'm innocent," she said. "Put it down to a mother's love. I was desperate at having Delilah taken away from me, taken just like that, without a word of explanation or farewell. I thought, well if they want to behave like that, so can I. I didn't kidnap her violently, I simply stole in to see her, lifted her gently in my arms and walked off with her."

"Without anyone's assistance."

"Cassandra, would Ben or April help me? After they'd slipped away to Barcelona like thieves?"

"What about Hamilton?"

"Hamilton would have no reason to help me."

I was puzzled. Surely if any of the three had facilitated the kidnap, now would be the time to betray them. Could it be someone else here in Barcelona? Someone I didn't know? It might have been lack of sleep, but I was starting to get a headache.

"Let's start at the beginning," I said. "You got into La Pedrera sometime when April was there alone, before I came over. You had scoped the place out earlier, and assuming you didn't have an accomplice who let you in, you bribed the *portero* to make you a key to their apartment. You went in, but before you could get Delilah, Hamilton and then Ben came home and you panicked. You rushed up to the roof where Ben cornered you, then came back downstairs and managed to grab Delilah and take her out to the street and find a taxi. All without help. You came to this hotel where you thought no one would find you, which is in a terrible neighborhood in case you hadn't noticed... so then what happened?"

"That's what I've been trying to tell you for the past fifteen minutes, Cassandra. You've been wasting valuable time with your accusations."

"I've just been trying to establish a chain of events," I said. "I have no reason in the world to help you, especially not after you've lied to me the way you have." I made as if to leave.

"Don't go," Frankie wailed and grabbed my arm. "I know I've lied to you. But I had no choice. You'd never have believed the truth."

"That's true," I said, sitting down next to her. "I wouldn't have, and maybe I still don't. Whatever the truth is."

"The important thing is that Delilah is missing. She's been missing for two hours already."

"When did you notice she was gone?"

"This morning. You know in these types of places they don't have a bathroom in the room but down the hall. About seven this morning Delilah got up and told me she was going to the bathroom. I was half asleep and hardly heard her and must have dropped off again. When I woke up it was eight-thirty and she wasn't in her bed. I thought she might have gotten lost in the hotel or be downstairs in the lobby, so I went rushing around trying to find her. She wasn't anywhere. That's when I called you."

I looked at my watch. It was nine-thirty. "Do you think she could have gone out in the street?" If she had there was no telling what could have happened to her.

But Frankie refused to believe that, perhaps because it was too horrible a thought, the idea of Delilah being picked up by thieves who might either try to ransom her or sell her. "I'm sure it was Ben," she said.

"But Ben had no idea where you'd taken Delilah," I said. "She thought you'd gone off to the airport and back to San

Francisco. We spent half the night there and at the train station."

"If only I had gone back to San Francisco," Frankie groaned.

"So how could Ben have known you were still here in Barcelona?"

"I told her."

"You told her!"

"Of course," Frankie said. "I'm not like her and April. I wouldn't want them to worry."

"Well, if you told them then why are you surprised they found you? Or came and got Delilah?"

"Because I didn't tell them where I was. There are hundreds of hotels in Barcelona. How could they have known it was this one?"

A good question. If I hadn't been able to find Frankie in the best hotels, how could Ben and April, who spoke little Spanish, have found Frankie in one of the worst hotels?

"I didn't even call them," said Frankie. "I sent a message with a taxi driver to their apartment. All it said was 'Delilah is safe with me. I will be contacting you soon to work out new custody arrangments.'"

I didn't know what to think. I preferred to think that April and Ben had somehow gotten the hotel's name from the taxi driver rather than that Delilah had been nabbed off the street by professional childnappers, but it was still all very confusing. If April and Ben knew where Delilah was why hadn't they contacted me? I'd searched out Hamilton last night, but he hadn't said a word. Perhaps they hadn't told him?

"Frankie," I said. "If you think Ben and April have Delilah and you know where they're staying, why don't you just go there and talk about it with them? What do you need me for?"

Frankie's thin lips quivered. "I need you to go with me."

"But why?"

"Because. Because I'm afraid of them." And Frankie burst into tears again.

◆

This was not the way I had envisioned my stay in Barcelona, speeding around in taxis with bereft mothers. Before I'd always taken this city at a leisurely pace: long mornings reading newspapers and books in cafés, which drifted into serious lunches with Ana and other friends; afternoons spent napping and strolling along the streets, stopping in bookstores and again in cafés; resplendent evenings full of food and music and talk.

Now I had the feeling that even Gaudí's architecture, which had always been a lovely backdrop for my wanderings, was never going to be the same for me.

We screeched up in front of the door to La Pedrera and went inside and up the elevator. Frankie was clutching my arm and smoking non-stop. My headache wasn't getting any better.

We knocked and April came to the door. She looked from me to Frankie with wide-open dark eyes. I couldn't read their expression. "Ben," she called, a little unsteadily. "Ben, they've brought Delilah back."

Then she noticed that Delilah wasn't with us, but not in time to warn Ben, who came rushing out of the shower with only a towel wrapped around her midriff. What's she got that I haven't, I thought. Except fifteen years or so and a tattoo of a dancing woman on her back shoulder.

"Where is she, where's Delilah?"

"I thought you had her," shrieked Frankie.

"Oh my god," said April. And fainted.

Neither Ben nor Frankie seemed to notice April's unconscious state, so it was left to me to bring her around with water from a vase of flowers, while Ben and Frankie screamed at each other. Or perhaps it was the screaming that brought her around.

"What have you done with Delilah?"

"Why are you pretending you don't have her?" Frankie grabbed Ben's arm and Ben's towel slipped off, revealing rock-hard thighs and an abdomen like a knotted slab of maple.

"April, April dear," I was murmuring. "Wake up April, are you all right? Do you want me to rub your feet?"

"You stole her right from under my very eyes and you think I have her?"

"You're the one who has her. You took her this morning when the poor little thing had to go to the bathroom."

"What are you talking about? I had no idea where you were. How could I have taken her?"

"I sent you a message. That's how you found me. Don't pretend you didn't get it."

April groaned and her eyelashes fluttered. I had to fight down a terrible desire to kiss her. April, I wanted to say, what are we doing with these two crazy people? Let's just you and me go away together, I know we're meant for each other. Her black eyes opened and she stared at me. According to the film script she should have murmured, "Darling, I knew it was you all the time." But instead she croaked, "Where am I?"

"You've always been like this," Ben shouted. "One lie after another, one excuse after another. I could give a damn if you'd had surgery to become an elephant, if only you'd be honest for once."

"You don't know a thing about honesty. Or human kindness. If you'd been honest or kind you never would have left San Francisco without telling me. Do you think it's been easy finding you? I had to give up my job, everything to follow you."

I assisted April to an upright position, but she seemed not to want to take part in the debate.

Frankie continued, "The only reason I took Delilah in the first place was to get you to agree to new custody arrangements."

"Kidnapping is no way to get me to agree to anything."

"Well, we're even now. I don't have Delilah and neither do you," Frankie said smugly. But then reality hit her. "Then she really has been kidnapped by white slave traders."

The two of them burst into shocked tears and then resumed accusing each other.

April said, "I think I need some fresh air."

◆

I walked April as gently as an invalid through the tiny Pasage de la Concepción that led from Gràcia to the Rambla de Catalunya, and seated her at an outdoor café sheltered from the sun. On either side of us traffic flashed by; it wasn't the quietest place for a conversation, but in Barcelona there aren't many quiet places. I often sat at this café, for it was just across from Ana's apartment building.

"Poor April," I said several times, encouragingly, but she only nodded her frizzy black hair. She looked a little older this morning, wearing a gold caftan that could have been a bathrobe, her darkly-haired legs shoved into Birkenstocks. I still adored her though.

I ordered tea and *ensaimadas*, the Catalan version of sweet turnovers.

"I feel so guilty," she said finally, in a low monotone. "Women are supposed to love kids, women are supposed to want kids, women are supposed to be crazy about babies and children. Well, I don't love kids, I mean, as a rule, as a *species*. And I can't stand how *central* children can be to someone's life, how parents can *fight* the way they do over a child."

"One thing I'll say for big Catholic families is that no one gets any special attention. The fighting was all between us when I was growing up." I paused. "Are you saying you don't like Delilah?"

"I *wanted* to like Delilah. . . . "

"But right from the beginning she was a bone of contention."

April shook her head. "I didn't even know that Ben had a daughter at first. I probably wouldn't have gotten involved with her if I'd known. But does she look like a mother?"

I had to shake my head. Out of the corner of my eye I saw the door to Ana's apartment building open and a large, brightly painted papier-maché arm protrude. Today Ana was taking her maternal construction to the home of the prospective mother.

"Of course she doesn't," said April, chewing on her sticky pastry. "She looks like a bodybuilder, she looks like a bulldyke, she looks like. . . "

"A boy."

"How was I supposed to know she had a daughter? She never mentioned her. It was all 'Oh, April you're the only one for me. April I'll love you till I die.' It was flowers and cards and phone calls until I gave in."

"And then you found out about Delilah. And Frankie."

"She wasn't only a mother, but a mother in a custody dispute. Not only a custody dispute, but a dispute about gender. About who was a real woman, who had the right to be the mother."

Ana, with her long braid tucked up under a workmanlike beret, was loading arms and legs into the back seat of the car she'd borrowed. She couldn't quite get the thighs to fit and had opened one of the back windows. The pair of red and yellow legs protruded wildly and disjointedly.

"Maybe I could have helped them," April said, as if to herself. "Maybe I could have gotten them to reconcile. But that would have meant committing myself to the relationship."

"And you couldn't," I said, "because there was Delilah."

"Exactly," she said.

"But then why did the three of you come to Barcelona to get away from Frankie?"

April had finished her *ensaimada* and was dabbing delicately at the plate with a finger. "That's what everyone thinks," she said. "But I came here by myself. Ben followed me. And let me tell you, it's been very difficult. I haven't had a moment's peace for a week."

Ana was struggling to fit the body's head into the passenger seat, where it sat, smiling benignly, like a totemic goddess. Something snapped into place. I stared at April in her rather tired caftan/bathrobe and for the first time her musky scents and freckled cleavage didn't overwhelm me.

"You drugged Delilah with some kind of herbal knock-out drops, didn't you? Then let Frankie in so she could kidnap her, didn't you? And then when I turned up at seven-thirty, you kept me occupied so you'd have an alibi, didn't you?"

April stared at me sadly. Her black hair looked grayer in the sunlight and her vibrant voice quavered. "I'm not a bad person. I'd never want you to think I'm a bad person."

"Didn't you think about how frightened Ben would be?"

"It was only going to be overnight, Frankie said. She wasn't going to take Delilah out of the city. It was a negotiating tool. I thought, I guess I thought that Ben needed to be scared. I guess I thought they'd all go back to San Francisco."

"How did Frankie persuade you? I thought you didn't like Frankie."

"I don't know if I do like Frankie," April said unhappily. "But it's not because of who she is or what she's become." She started to cry. "It's all so complicated. You'd never understand. And now Delilah's really gone."

"Then there's no possibility that Ben really did steal Delilah out of the hotel this morning?"

"Ben and I slept until nine-thirty. We were exhausted, we'd been up half the night."

"But Frankie sent a message that Delilah was safe."

"That's a message we never got."

"Why *is* Hamilton so suspicious of you?"

That shook April up. "What makes you think he's suspicious of me?"

"He didn't want to let you out of his sight all last night."

"He's not suspicious of me. We're old friends."

"Since when?"

"Since high school. We... played in the orchestra together."

"Where was that?"

"Just what is your point, Cassandra?" A harshness I'd never heard before came into April's voice. She set her cup of tea down with a clatter.

"My point is that there's something funny going on between you and Hamilton."

"You're the one who's suspicious," she turned it on me. "Working for Frankie, hounding us to Barcelona. You'd be the likeliest to have taken Delilah this morning. It's something

125

Frankie cooked up, I'm sure of it. Pretending that Delilah was kidnapped when Frankie has just got her stashed somewhere."

For a second her guess rang true. God, it was just the kind of thing that Frankie might do. But then I remembered Frankie's anguish in the hotel. She couldn't fake that, could she?

"Are you ready to go back to La Pedrera and talk about this sensibly?" I asked instead.

"You go," she said, struggling for serenity. "I need a little time alone. This fighting between Frankie and Ben may not be old to you, but it is to me. I can't face it."

"You can't pretend all this isn't happening, April," I said. "Delilah is gone, and naturally Frankie and Ben are upset. They're her parents."

"I know," she said. After a minute she added, "There's something I'd like to tell you, but not right now. Could you give me a couple hours to work up to it? We could meet for lunch at the market off the Ramblas, the Mercat Sant Josep. There's a restaurant there, Hamilton took me once."

"I'm not sure I should let you out of my sight," I said. "Why can't you tell me now?"

"Because. . . " Her voice changed. "What's that? Somebody is running down the street with a. . . a head."

I followed her pointing finger. Ana had left the car unlocked while she went back upstairs to get more body parts and someone, a young boy, was indeed dashing across the Rambla de Catalunya with the peacefully smiling red and yellow papier-maché head of Ana's birthing house.

I jumped up from my chair and tore after him, but he was too quick for me. I chased him down the center walkway, but lost him in the end down a side street.

Ana was standing by the car when I returned empty-handed. A small crowd of passersby and neighbors had gathered to tell her what had happened and to discuss, in very loud voices, how things were going to the dogs in Barcelona. Now they were stealing art, right out of cars!

"The head's not the important bit," I tried to reassure Ana. "Many women become mothers without using their heads."

"I'm late," Ana snapped, slamming the door of the car and driving off in a temper.

I turned back to the café and the foot masseuse of my dreams. Perhaps I shouldn't have been surprised.

April was gone.

14

I was on my way through the Pasage de la Concepción back to
La Pedrera when I recognized Ben and Frankie coming towards
me. Ben had pulled on jeans and a sweatshirt with the name of
some gym in San Francisco, and she was marching ahead of
Frankie through the little pedestrian street. They were still
quarrelling.

"I don't understand how you could accept me once with all
my quirks and eccentricities and then go so judgmental on me,"
Frankie was saying. In contrast to Ben who set each high-top
sneaker down as if it were a dumbbell, Frankie bounced and slid
along in her pointed shoes.

"We didn't have anybody else in Iowa," Ben said glumly.
"We had to accept each other."

"I'm no different than what I was ten years ago."

Ben turned on her. "You're completely different, Frankie.
How can you say you're not different?"

Frankie stopped too. "Aren't you ever going to understand? I
never was a man. Never felt like one, never looked like one,
never was one inside. I was always a woman."

"You didn't feel to me like a woman."

"What do you know and what does it matter anyway?"
Frankie's triangular face twisted sadly. "I thought you loved me
for the person I was and am. My qualities have never changed
even though my body did."

"I do care about you, Frankie," Ben said, after a minute.
"But I don't know how to deal with you anymore."

"Sometimes I think that my caring about Delilah throws your whole self-concept of motherhood in doubt. If I can be a mother too, what does your motherhood mean?"

"There's always one biological mother," Ben said. "That's the way it is. And the biological mother always feels different than the other parent."

"I don't believe that," said Frankie. "Motherhood isn't about biology, it's about love."

"Don't talk to me about biology meaning nothing," Ben snapped, starting to walk away again. "We are our bodies, our bodies make us who we are. You can't just play fast and loose with biology."

"Says the great bodybuilder," Frankie said snidely.

They both saw me.

"Where's April?" Ben demanded.

"I . . . well . . . I don't know exactly."

Frankie looked closely at me and then rolled her eyes nervously.

"What's wrong, where's April?" Ben repeated, advancing on me threateningly, "I know you've been seeing her. What's going on between you?"

It's hard to tell someone that their lover has betrayed them, no matter what that betrayal consists of.

But Frankie took the initiative. "Look, Ben, you had to know sometime. April helped me with Delilah last night."

"I don't believe you!"

"It's true, Ben," I said. "Frankie set it up with April to let her into the apartment while I was there, so that she'd have an alibi. But Hamilton came home and then you did, and . . . you know the rest."

"I don't believe you," Ben said again, her solid face anguished. "Why would April do such a thing to me? She loves me, she loves Delilah, she was the one who set up this whole trip to Barcelona . . . Cassandra, you're in on this with Frankie, you're making this up."

Frankie's voice shook, "Can't you get it through your head that April doesn't like kids?"

"I'm afraid it's true, Ben," I said. "April told me as much out on the street. She doesn't feel comfortable around kids. And she says you followed her to Barcelona."

"April would never say that!"

"Is it or isn't it true?" Frankie demanded. "Is that why you took Delilah out of school, quit your job and disrupted all our lives? Because of some half-baked infatuation with a foot therapist?"

"Oh, what does it matter," Ben wailed, "when Delilah's gone." She turned on Frankie. "It's all your fault. If you hadn't come here and stirred up trouble, none of this would have happened. April and I were making progress on our relationship. Now she's gone."

"She's gone and she's taken Delilah with her," said Frankie portentously. "She stole our daughter from the hotel this morning."

"How do you know that, Frankie?"

"Who else could it be?"

I tried to get things back to a level of rationality. "What reason would April have for taking Delilah, Frankie?"

"You think she did too, admit it!"

"Well, she did say she had something to tell me. We agreed to meet in an hour at the restaurant inside the Mercat Sant Josep. Maybe she felt bad about having helped last night."

"But she fainted today when you two showed up without Delilah," Ben said. "Doesn't that prove she's innocent?"

"Maybe she's just high-strung," Frankie said. "Those spiritual types often are."

"April told me you slept in until nine-thirty, Ben. Wouldn't you have noticed if she'd gone out?"

"She's been sleeping in a different room," Ben said painfully. "We don't sleep together."

But that admission must have been too much for her. Because right after she made it she ran back the way she'd come to the Passeig de Gràcia and jumped into a passing cab.

"Come on," Frankie said, taking my arm, "Talk to me."

◆

We sat down at April's and my old seats at the outdoor table, and ordered *cafés con leche.*

"Do you really think April has Delilah then?" Frankie said anxiously, lighting up a Camel.

"I hope so."

Frankie sighed. "Ben and her girlfriends! And she says *I'm* unstable." She crossed her legs and struck a wounded pose. "She talks about my lying! I'm an amateur next to her. Can you believe we're all here in Barcelona because Ben has a *crush* on someone?"

I had to smile. "So what did you say to April yesterday afternoon to persuade her to help you?"

Frankie put a finger to her red lips. "I have my ways."

"Did you offer her money? Did you blackmail her?"

"Did I threaten to expose her as practicing Reflexology under false pretenses? No, I simply suggested that I could take Delilah off her hands for a while. You see, even in San Francisco I'd noticed that April was never very happy to see Delilah when I dropped her off after a weekend."

The waitress crossed the street from the bar on the corner with our coffee.

Frankie was already wired. She kept talking. "To hear Ben go on you'd think it was totally her idea to have Delilah and totally her responsibility. But it was *my* idea. I was the one who wanted a child."

"Ben said you met in college."

"We did, we were inseparable. We were roommates for two years and then we got married. You couldn't pry us apart."

"How could she have not known about you? How could you have not known about each other?"

"I said we were *close.* I didn't say we ever *talked.* For christssake, we were eighteen when we met, twenty-one when we had Delilah. I didn't have a clue who I was. Yes, I had these *feelings* but I thought they'd go away. They didn't and I'm happy they didn't. I'm just starting my life in some ways and it's exciting. I'm living my life finally as I want to live it. But that doesn't mean I don't have a right to be a mother. I am a parent.

I have a child. And nobody can take her away from me."

"Frankie, you and Ben have to work this stuff out. It isn't good for Delilah."

"Ben and her girlfriends aren't good for Delilah," she said stubbornly. "Delilah and I are fine together."

"What about you, don't you have a relationship?"

"Not at the moment," she said. "Someday I'll find the right man. I'm not like Ben. When I get attached, I stay attached."

Speaking of attachments. . .

The head was coming down the street on two blue-jeaned legs. She was still smiling implacably.

"Excuse me," I said, and pelted across the street. It wasn't my physical prowess but luck and caffeine that enabled me to grab the teenage boy. Plus the fact that he wasn't running.

"Where do you think you're going, *ladrón?*" I shouted.

But he wasn't really a pickpocket, just a university student who'd been having second thoughts.

"I thought it might look good in my room," he apologized. "I'm really very sorry. I wanted to bring it back to where I took it from."

He handed it over to me with a sheepish look and I hadn't the heart to scold him.

"Mom's back!" I turned to call to Frankie, but she was no longer there.

The Mercat Sant Josep was a nineteenth-century enclosed marketplace of glass and wrought iron, of the train-station school of architecture. A little city of comestibles: houses built of oranges and bananas; monuments of dried apricots and peaches; parks of leafy greens and browns. The cheese sellers stood behind cases of fresh white *queso de Burgos* and hard yellowish chunks from the Pyrenees; they would thinly slice you a hundred grams, if you asked, of salty Serrano ham, or cut you off a chunk of sausage or sell you a whole strand of fatty rust-red chorizo. I always avoided the meat displays with their plucked chickens dangling from the top of the stand like traitors on a gibbet, but I often was drawn, as if by undersea currents, to the icy stands of fish, where the fishmongers looked as pale as their catch from long years of sunless filleting and wrapping.

In the restaurant inside the market I took a seat that faced the window and ordered a three-course lunch of salad, braised lamb with fried potatoes and *crema catalana* for dessert. There was no sign of April.

I took a long time to eat. I had a small carafe of wine and then coffee. I watched the vegetable sellers outside the restaurant strip the soiled outer leaves from a boxful of lettuce, build a barricade of potatoes against an encroachment of rocket-shaped parsnips, fling limp carrots with seaweed-like hair back into the bin. After a while I noticed someone standing outside the restaurant and staring in. He was wearing a turtleneck sweater and a suede jacket; his hair was pulled back in a ponytail and he had on very dark Italian shades. He smoked with the cigarette held between his thumb and forefinger.

I'd seen him somewhere... and a shiver went up my spine. Maybe he was the man who'd followed me through the Barri Gòtic. A professional thief—or someone Frankie or Ben or even April had hired to stake me out and kill me.

For he was definitely staking someone out. I glanced covertly around the restaurant. Was there anyone here I'd missed? The small room was packed and the waiters dashed expertly back and forth from the kitchen with plates of food and bottles of wine.

Then I saw that the tough didn't have his eye on me, but on an elderly woman seated at the bar in front of the restaurant. I wasn't surprised I hadn't noticed her before. In her black head scarf, black dress and black shawl she looked like a widow who'd wandered in from the countryside to see a big-city relative. She was perched on a stool at the bar eating a sandwich and drinking mineral water, with her head down and her eyes moving restlessly.

There was something peculiar about those eyes.

They were blue.

In my surprise I knocked over my water carafe, and when I

looked up again, she was gone. So was the tough guy in the suede jacket. I hastily paid my bill and ran out of the restaurant in search of them.

It was two o'clock, *siesta* time, and some of the stands were closed, while others had been left in the care of a son or a daughter. There were a couple of men pushing brooms around and not many customers.

There she was, the little old lady in black. But how oddly she walked, not as if she were old, and not as if she were a lady either. Was she Hamilton in drag? I flattened myself against a stand with its metal door rolled down and let the *señora* cross the aisle perpendicular to mine. A few seconds later the man in the dark glasses slid past, smooth and soundless as a fish in an aquarium. He had a leather bag over one shoulder. Yes, it *was* him—the man with the threatening sack who'd followed me through the Barri Gòtic from the Ramblas and scared the wits out of me.

I squeezed into a tiny space between two stands and waited till he'd passed by.

The afternoon light filtered in through the dusty windows overhead and an eerie quiet seemed to blanket the great hall. A sensation of dread spread through my limbs and my heart pounded. I had the distinct impression that I was going to witness something awful.

A scream cut the air.

I rounded the corner at a bound to see the widow and the tough locked in a death grip, rolling on the floor on a rapidly flattening cushion of bananas which they must have knocked over when they began to grapple.

"Stop it, stop it," a teenage girl in a green apron was crying. She told me and the others who converged upon the stand, "They just started fighting, I don't know why."

"*Mira,* it's two men," someone said, trying to tear them apart.

"*No, son dos mujeres,*" someone else said.

The widow's black scarf had fallen away, revealing a blond brush cut, and the tough's dark glasses had smashed in pieces.

The two struggling bodies were smeared with banana mush; that suede jacket would never be the same.

"*Son maridos*," I explained. Married. And some of the crowd, at least, seemed to understand. "Well actually," I admitted. "They're divorced."

Ben was the first to recover. "You said April would be here with Delilah," she accused me.

"I guess I was wrong."

Frankie undid her ponytail and lit a cigarette. "You look totally ridiculous, Ben. Even before I had my operation I could do a better job of passing than that."

Ben angrily tore off her shawl. Her biceps strained at the thin fabric over her shoulders.

"What have I done to you, Frankie, that you should be following me like this?"

"You thought you could just come to the restaurant and take Delilah off with you."

"Well, isn't that what you thought?"

"Frankie, Ben," I pleaded. "Your daughter's missing. What's it going to take for you to be seriously worried?"

"You shut up, Cassandra," Ben said, and she flung her shawl over her shoulder as she stomped off down the aisle. "What do you know about anything? You've never even been a mother."

What a rejoinder. I was dumbstruck.

"Wait Ben," Frankie called. "I'm coming with you, like it or not."

"I take it I'm definitely fired then?" I shouted after Frankie.

But neither of them bothered to reply.

15

Now there was always the possibility that April had been run over by a moving vehicle while deep in thought as poor Mr. Gaudí had been by the tram, and that she was lying in a hospital somewhere without her identification or her wits. There was the possibility that she had fallen asleep on a park bench, or broken the law and been carted off to jail, or even that someone in our small circle had done away with her.

But I thought the likeliest thing was that April had simply tricked me and I had fallen for it. Why bother to hide anything when you can simply hide?

I retraced a path to the Hotel Palacio and went back up the grimy stairs to the lobby. One of the sisters was sitting motionless behind the counter. At first I thought she had fallen asleep and simply forgotten to close her eyes, but she snorted out a hostile "*Sí, señor?*" to let me know I wasn't going to get away with anything here.

I disregarded the *señor* and asked politely if she'd been working here this morning when the little girl had gone missing.

"I didn't see anything," she said. She was one of those old women who wither rather than softly expand, and on her cheek she had a big black mole with long gray hairs.

I flipped open my wallet to show my London tube pass. "INTERPOL," I said briefly. "We're working on a tip from the Guardia Civil. A six-year-old Irish girl was abducted from her home in Dublin yesterday by either the IRA or the UDA. She's the daughter of the prime minister. We've traced her to this hotel."

The *señora*'s eyes didn't blink. "I didn't see anything."

"Do you know the penalty for lying to an INTERPOL agent?"

"*No vi nada,*" she repeated.

Stronger action was required. I took out my wallet again and put a thousand-peseta note on the counter. She looked at it. I placed another on top. She reached for them.

"Not so fast, *señora.* Do you know the penalty for accepting a bribe?"

She put on a crafty senile expression and began to babble incoherently—something about mothers, I thought, but it was in Catalan, so I couldn't tell. Her sister, who had an identical mole, only on her forehead, came out of a back room and demanded to know what was going on.

I forewent the INTERPOL story and simply pointed to the pesetas on the counter. "Who took the little girl this morning?"

"A woman who said she was her mother," the sister said.

If it was Ben I'd kill her. But we already knew that Ben would have a hard time passing as female.

"Was she a large woman?"

The two sisters looked at each other. They nodded.

Well at least I knew now it was April.

"Did she say where she was taking the little girl?"

As one they shook their tiny shrunken heads.

Considering the first sister had addressed me as *señor* I didn't put much stock in their answer, but I asked it anyway. "You're sure the lady was a woman?"

"*Sí, sí, madres son mujeres, claro,*" the second sister said firmly, as if I were an idiot.

I guessed she had a point. Mothers were women. At least they used to be.

In the back of my mind I'd been harboring a suspicion of Hamilton. How much more convenient it would be if he were involved. But the *señora*'s answer left me in no doubt: April had come to the hotel this morning and taken Delilah.

The question was, what had she done with her? Another hotel seemed likeliest. But where?

The hot spring sun beat down on me and suddenly I felt rather faint. It's hard work looking for people and that's why I'd never been good at Ditchum. I hate hard work.

I noticed a shoeshine stand next door to the Hotel Palacio and went inside.

"*Señor.*" He showed me a seat with a flourish.

I sighed and told him to give my boots a good shine. I wondered if this was how Frankie had felt when, as a boy who firmly believed he was a girl, everyone had treated him as a boy.

The *limpiabotas* was an old guy of about seventy who must have seen a lot from this shoeshine stand over the years. The civil war, the Franco years, the change to social democracy. I wondered if he'd seen April and Delilah this morning.

"How early do you open?" I asked.

"*Temprano.* It's the best time for me early in the morning when people are going to work."

"Did you happen to see a fat woman and a little girl, a blond-haired girl about six, come out of the hotel this morning?"

He thought about it. "I saw a little boy and his mother come out of the hotel, but the *señora* was not fat."

"You're sure it was a little boy?"

"*Sí, sí.*"

It was one thing to call me sir but to mistake Delilah with her pigtails and dresses for a boy, no, that was impossible. Plus, April was a big woman. The sisters had noticed it.

"Thanks anyway," I said, giving him a tip, and walked back to the Ramblas.

It was about three, mid-*siesta,* and I suddenly felt too tired to think. I took the metro from Liceu to Diagonal and went straight to my room at Ana's and lay down in bed. There I fell into a deep sleep.

I dreamed that I was floating along the river in the jungle on a small raft and that the lianas embraced over me, shutting out most of the sun. It was cool and dark emerald green. Blood red parrots chattered overhead, in a language I could almost understand, Catalan perhaps. At first it was pleasant to lie there, floating along, but after a while I began to be anxious. I remembered I was supposed to be looking for someone. From time to time I would pass a hut or something that looked like a hut, but the jungle was dense and the river carried me along quickly; when I cried out no one answered.

Finally, just as twilight deepened the gloom of the jungle even more, just as I began to be really worried, I came in sight of a settlement. As I floated past it I yelled in Spanish, "I am Cristobel's daughter," and immediately people began to come out of the huts, to get into their canoes. Five or six of them paddled towards me. I kept saying, "I'm Cristobel's long-lost daughter," until I realized they couldn't understand me and that, in fact, they were probably going to have me for dinner or worse.

They weren't women and they weren't men, these villagers. As they grabbed my raft and secured it with ropes to their canoes, I asked stupidly (considering I believed my life in danger), "Has your village ever been featured in *National Geographic*? Somehow I don't remember it."

"Uga-muga," they said.

They had breasts, but they had penises too; their lank brown hair was long and they had bones in their flat noses. Their eyes were uncivilized and hostile. I hope they don't try any hankypanky with me, I worried as they dragged me back to their camp.

The settlement was lit by bonfires and a huge old person was waiting for me with an expression of great disbelief. This person instructed the villagers to undress me. I resisted, less out of modesty than because I had a feeling they were probably going to eat me at some point during the evening, but they prevailed. I was forced to sit in front of this enormous hermaphrodite. Meanwhile the villagers were making rude noises and pointing at my missing appendage.

I tried to explain that María had made me take this journey and that I was looking for my mother, I mean my daughter, but I realized that being both sexes as they were they might not understand the intensely proprietal relationship between mothers and daughters. I didn't, in fact, see any children about. The hermaphrodite silenced me with a wave of a torch he/she had been handed. Oh god, now the torture was going to start, I knew it. The huge being took one of my feet in her/his hands and began to stroke my sole with fire.

"It's funny," I said. "That doesn't feel so bad," but the fire got hotter and hotter, the hermaphrodite's eyes burned into me, there was something wrong here. . . .

"Cassandra," said Ana. "Telephone."

"Thank god you woke me up," I said, shaking my head dazedly. "I was in a jungle, they were going to eat me, they didn't understand Spanish, they were doing something to my feet."

Ana shook my shoulder, "Wake up, Cassandra. Ben is on the telephone."

I staggered out to the living room. I was never going to consume a big lunch and take a *siesta* again. Who were those people, what was it all about?

As if she hadn't stomped away from me in a fury not two hours ago Ben asked, "Did you find April?"

I still hadn't quite gotten out of the jungle and back to Barcelona. "April?"

"Did April turn up at the market with Delilah?"

"Oh. April. Oh. Delilah. Oh. No."

"Cassandra—what happened?"

"April never showed up so I went back to the hotel where Frankie had been staying and questioned the women at the desk, and they finally said that a woman who said she was Delilah's mother took her early this morning."

Ben dropped the phone and started screaming, "Frankie, you've been fucking me over again. You made up the story,

Cassandra says. You stole Delilah from yourself!"

In vain I tried to talk to the dangling receiver, "Ben, no, listen. It was April. April who took Delilah. And April who's disappeared."

Frankie got on the phone. "Cassandra, you're lying!" she screamed. "You were there with me this morning, you saw how upset I was. Why are you making this up?"

"Frankie, wait," I said, but she had dropped the receiver too. I could hear the two of them shouting at each other.

There was nothing to do but hang up and wait till they called me back.

Ana had been listening to all this.

"You mean they've lost their little girl again?" she asked.

"Well, I think April has her now," I said. "April is the foot masseuse I told you about."

Ana shook her head. "All women want children," she said glumly.

"Except me and April," I said. "That's why I'm worried."

"Don't worry," said Ana, "If you could find my head this morning you can surely find a little girl." She took my arm. "Come," she said. "Look at the new house I'm building."

She led me into the workroom where a cluster of amoeba-like shapes lay about.

"What is it?" I asked.

"I don't know," Ana admitted. "But you spending so much time at La Pedrera has made me start thinking about Gaudí again. Everything I've been doing has been so representational —I thought I'd like to work with organic form again. To get away from the same old boxes."

She picked up one of the shapes. "These are fiberglass. My idea is that they would be lined with some soft material and that they could clip together in some way, possibly Velcro, so that the child could create the house herself. Sometimes it could be small or narrow, sometimes very open and big. It could have many rooms or few rooms. When she travelled she could take a part of it with her perhaps. Or make a doll house from some of it or a little cave where she could curl up and read."

She flipped her long braid over her shoulder. "I'm very enthusiastic about it. About the shapes it could take. And how a child might use it."

The phone rang again.

I answered it cautiously. It was Frankie. "Cassandra, I demand an apology."

"Look, I never *said* that you were lying about this morning. All I said was that the two women at the desk maintained that a woman pretending to be Delilah's mother took her. It must have been someone Delilah knew, therefore I'm guessing it was April. But that's what I already suspected."

"But why hasn't April brought Delilah back? Why hasn't she contacted us?"

"I don't know," I said. "Have you asked Hamilton?"

"Why would Hamilton know anything about this?"

"He might know something about April that we don't."

Ben took the phone. "What did you say about Hamilton?"

"I said, I think there's more to Hamilton than meets the eye."

"That's ridiculous, Cassandra. He's been suspicious of *you*, that's his only interest in all this."

"I know," I said. "That's why I'm suspicious of him."

"Look, you've got to find Delilah."

"Maybe it's time to call the police."

"How the hell would we explain all this in Catalan?"

She had a point. "Call the American consulate. They can help."

"You think they're going to be more sympathetic to people like us?"

"Don't you pay taxes like everyone else?"

"Well, I pay taxes. Frankie doesn't."

"You're American citizens who've lost their daughter. You have a right to get help."

"Cassandra—"

"Look, I'm not your mother." The fatal word slipped out.

"And you don't have any idea of what it is to be a mother either."

Frankie grabbed the phone. "And after all the money I paid you."

"I'll be in touch," I said coolly and hung up.

"That's good, Cassandra," Ana said. "It's their problem. Let them figure it out."

"Yeah," I said. I wondered why I didn't really trust them to figure anything out, much less do anything about it. They were probably back to shouting blame at each other right now.

"Ana," I said. "What do you think, do you want to take a little trip to the Barri Gòtic on your *moto*?"

16

It was about seven o'clock, a late afternoon hour that rubs up against the edges of the evening—not exactly twilight, with the violet gloom that word conjures up, nor sunset with its frets of rose and gold, but a time of darkening greenery and feverish sweetness, when the stale afternoon air somehow manages to refresh itself and the electric lights going on one by one suggest excitement and splendor beyond their modest wattage.

Sitting behind Ana on the *moto* was always an exhilarating, if hair-raising experience. Her intellectual airs vanished and a new persona, fierce and warrior-like, appeared, ready to cut in front of taxis, to narrowly avoid mowing down pedestrians, to roar up onto the sidewalk to escape a traffic jam. We sped down Gràcia in an exuberant roar and winged around the fountains of the Plaça de Catalunya. We should have been wearing helmets, but it felt so good with nothing between us and the fresh green air of spring. Then it was down the Via Laietana, swarming with traffic but with its spectacular views of the old Roman walls and the bell tower of the cathedral rising up behind, fantastically illuminated like something out of a medieval dream, and into the Barri Gòtic where we whizzed like angels on a mission through the Plaça de Sant Jaume. Here Ana only just avoided disembowelling a Japanese tourist and I thought, I never want to leave Barcelona, I always want to be here. The ancient cobbled square was ringed with massive government buildings from the Renaissance, lit from below so they almost seemed to float suspended above the plaza. But before I could tell Ana I'd decided to stay forever, the romantic square had given way to streets of shops and pedestrians who dared us to kill them. Straight down Carrer de Ferran and onto D'Avinyo, deep into the *barrio* we zoomed, until I pointed—It's there—then Ana braked sharply and returned to her unruffled calm.

"It looks closed."

"I don't think it opens until later."

I got stiffly off the *moto* and forced myself back to the business at hand. I banged on the rolling aluminum door. There was no answer.

"Let's go around back," Ana suggested.

We explored the narrow street behind the jazz club, and found a kitchen entrance. The door was unlocked, and we went in. From somewhere inside came the cool, deliberate riffs of an alto sax, like water cascading in rivulets and droplets over a high precipice.

We were in a dim cluttered hallway that smelled of stale cigarette smoke and faintly of urine; the walls were a peeling whitewash over which had been plastered old jazz posters and newspaper clippings. It was all quite different from the glossy hightech club room in front. Hamilton must be practicing up there, and maybe, just maybe, April had told him something that I wanted to know.

I gestured to Ana to follow me, but she was staring curiously at the news clippings and posters. I could see her acquisitive mind at work, wondering what treasures she could unearth in the back rooms of this old jazz club. She opened a door in the corridor and we found the performers' lounge with lot of unwashed coffee cups and stained towels lying about. Another door proved to have a toilet and storage space behind it and a third yielded a kitchen.

In the kitchen, a wizened old cook was playing a game of cards with a small blond girl.

"Well. What do you know," I said. "Fancy meeting you here."

"Hi," Delilah said warily. You could see from her eyes, behind her serious-looking glasses, that she was wondering, What next?

I said, "Do you remember me, Delilah?"

"Yes," she said. "You came to the park."

"That's right," I said. "I'm a friend of your mother and your. . . Frankie."

She shot me a look. "Nobody is a friend of both Ben and Frankie."

"Let's just say that first I knew Frankie and then I got to know Ben and April."

We introduced each other all round. Ana asked the cook in Catalan where Delilah had come from. He shrugged his shoulder in the direction of the sax.

"What are they saying?" Delilah asked me.

"They're wondering who that lady was who came and got you from the hotel this morning."

Delilah smiled with her still-perfect baby teeth. She was wearing a pair of jeans and a tee-shirt that said Yo ♥ Barcelona. Her blond pigtails had been caught up under a Giants baseball cap and she had a smear of chocolate on one cheek.

"That was no lady," she said. "It was Hamilton."

"Hamilton?" I said. "I thought it was April."

Delilah sighed and shook her head violently. "It was Hamilton. He was wearing a dress."

"A dress!!"

"And a wig." Delilah wrinkled her nose. I knew where she'd gotten that from. "And too much make-up."

"Delilah, didn't you think that Frankie might be worried when you didn't come back to the room?"

"Hamilton said he would tell Frankie. . . didn't he?"

"Not exactly," I said. "In fact, neither Ben nor Frankie knows where you are."

Delilah stopped shuffling her cards an instant. She sighed, and chewed a little on one of her small fingernails. At six she'd already had to learn to submit to the whimsical universe of adults and to be diplomatic about it. It was a lot of responsibility.

"Are you going to tell them where I am?" she finally asked, carefully.

"I will if you want me to," I said. "I think they're worried about you. I think they'd like to know you're safe."

I thought back to Frankie and Ben quarrelling furiously at La Pedrera. Blaming each other had been more on their minds than worrying about where Delilah was. I wanted to think that they only quarrelled because they loved their daughter.

"What do you think, Delilah," I said. "Do you want to stay in Barcelona or go back to San Francisco?"

"I was in the first grade," she said. "They just took me out. I liked school. I had friends."

"I know your parents just want what's best for you."

"I know three kids that are AIs," she said. "That's artificially inseminated. They don't have fathers, one has two women mothers and the other kids just have one mother. Nobody has what I have."

"What do you think about what you have?"

"Well," she considered. "I like my mom, except when she's tired and in a bad mood. Frankie is always in a good mood, but I don't see her that much. I like her too. They're my parents, you know."

"What about April?"

Delilah sighed again and devoted herself to the game.

I repeated, "What about April?"

"She doesn't like me, I don't think."

"Why do you think that is?"

"I don't know... maybe because... " Delilah stopped and looked behind me.

"Oh hello," I said, and to Ana, "Another mother."

Hamilton came into the kitchen.

"I thought I heard voices," he said mildly, not at all embarrassed to have been discovered as a childnapper.

"How could you?" I said. "You knew how worried Ben would be. And Frankie. And how did you know where Frankie's hotel was anyway?"

"I think I'd like to talk about this elsewhere," he said meaningfully.

We left Ana to join in on the card game, and Hamilton led the way back to the large room where he'd been practicing among the black lacquer tables piled with chairs.

"And wearing a dress," I said. "What put that in your head?"

"Sit down," Hamilton said. He himself perched on a table. His sax gleamed dully in a corner of the darkening room. There was still a little light from the windows and he hadn't put the overhead lamps on yet. He was looking serious and masculine but I could still see traces of pancake make-up on his roundish face and touches of mascara on his lashes.

"Tell me about your childhood, Cassandra."

"*What?*"

"Did you have two parents, a brother or sister, a nice home in the suburbs?"

"I had a widowed mother, a pack of obnoxious siblings, a falling-down house in Kalamazoo, Michigan, and what's it to you?"

"My family had money," he said. "But my parents hated each other. They made my childhood hell, always fighting over me, always trying to get me to say I liked Mother better, or that I wanted to stay with Father."

"That's too bad," I said, fidgeting.

"We lived in Manhattan. Father lived uptown, Mother lived in the Village. My father was convinced my mother was a slut and a bohemian; my mother thought my father was a dull old fart. I was their only child; eventually Mother remarried but Father stayed a bachelor. I haven't seen them for years. I can't forgive them."

"What are you trying to tell me, Hamilton?"

"I'm trying to tell you that I know what it's like to be the child of divorced parents."

Hamilton bowed his head so that his receding hairline took on a tender, vulnerable edge.

"I hated to see Frankie and Ben quarrelling about Delilah. I thought maybe if I took Delilah myself they'd see how foolish they were being."

149

"But how'd you know where Frankie was?"

"She's not very smart really," he said. "She sent a taxi driver with a message that Delilah was okay. I had the *portero* hold him until I got downstairs, then I gave the driver a large tip and got the name of the hotel."

"At least Frankie thought to tell Ben that Delilah was okay."

"Ouch."

"When did the taxi driver show up?"

"While you and Ben were at the airport."

"So April knew where Frankie was keeping Delilah?"

"No." But his eyes slid away.

"She did know. That's why she's hiding from me."

"What do you mean she's hiding?"

"I mean that April got me to help her slip away from La Pedrera this morning to confess to me that she'd helped Frankie abduct Delilah. Then she said she had something to tell me, and agreed to meet me later for lunch. But when I turned up she wasn't there. Nobody knows where she is."

"She said she had something to tell you?"

"Probably that you'd taken Delilah, right? You two must have hatched this plan while Ben and I were at the airport last night. She wanted Delilah out of the way and you agreed to help her. Don't give me all this bull about divorced parents and lonely children."

"But it's true." Hamilton looked depressed. He got down from the table and walked around the room. "I wonder what April's up to."

"Who cares? The important thing is to get Delilah back to Ben and Frankie. They're worried sick."

"No," Hamilton said, and looked at me. "Please, Cassandra. Let me talk to them, please. Otherwise you know how it will go. They'll be at each other's throats, and Delilah will keep suffering. Let me arrange a meeting with them tomorrow morning. A healthy, calm meeting where we'll lay all the issues on the table and discuss them like rational adults."

"You call them then and tell them that you have Delilah. Right now."

Without further argument Hamilton moved to the phone and dialled. The room was almost completely dark now and Hamilton seemed shadowy and insubstantial, almost pathetic. I needed to remember that he wasn't just the lonely and fought-over child, but a competent adult, capable of love and music and even great deviousness.

"Ben," he said. "It's me, Hamilton. Look, I don't want you to worry, but Delilah's with me. Yes, I know. Yes. Yes. I'm really sorry. It seemed like the best thing. Listen, please, now don't get upset, Ben. I want to have a meeting with you and Frankie. I think we need to have a talk about the effect all this fighting is having on Delilah. I'm really concerned. Now don't yell at me. I'm only doing what I think is best, no I'm not going to tell you where she is yet. Is Frankie there? Good. The two of you need to sit down and really talk. I want you to talk, not just call each other names. I'll call you later, and if you haven't made any progress tonight I'll keep Delilah until tomorrow. Don't yell, Ben."

He hung up. "That woman has a loud voice." He turned on the overhead lamps and the room was flooded with light.

"But she agreed?"

"She wasn't happy about it, but yes, she agreed. I guess she knows that she and Frankie can't go on like this. That they need an outside mediator."

"Didn't she ask where April was?"

"Maybe April's back at La Pedrera."

"I don't know about April," I shook my head.

"What do you mean?"

"You know, first of all, it's really hard for me to believe that you and April are old friends. You just don't seem the type."

Hamilton shrugged. "What type is that? We were close as. . . once. There's a basic loyalty there."

I scrutinized him through narrowed eyes. "Just don't be fucking me over, Hamilton."

"You're one tough lady, you know that."

"Speaking of ladies—"

"You mean me? Yes, I crossdress sometimes. I've done it all

my life and I enjoy it." He looked at me a bit defiantly. "I find that wearing women's clothing gives me access to the feminine part of myself, to the softer, gentler aspects of my personality. It's hard being a man, Cassandra."

"So I've heard."

"You'd be surprised, Cassandra, at the cues people pick up on to distinguish gender. Crossdressing throws our rigid dualistic thinking into chaos. It's very liberating. You should try it sometime."

"Just call me *señor*."

We went back into the kitchen where Ana and Delilah were getting on splendidly, drawing pictures of dinosaurs on butcher paper. Hamilton sat down with them and picked up a brown crayon. "I can draw a pretty good stegosaurus, want to see?"

"Yes!" said Delilah happily.

I guessed I didn't need to worry about her for the time being.

"Is there a phone here I can use?"

The cook pointed to the hallway.

I reached Carmen at the salon, and asked her the Spanish equivalent of "What's shakin', baby?"

"Cassandra! My mother had to go back to Granada suddenly. One of our relatives is ill."

"Oh, that's too bad," I said, wondering why she was telling me. "Do you want to cancel our date?"

"Cancel?" she said, affronted, and was silent.

Oh why was my Carmen such a moody, mysterious woman? Then it suddenly hit me.

"Do you mean I can come over to your house?"

"*Sí.*"

"Do you mean your mother won't be there?"

"*Sí.*"

"Do you mean what I think you mean?"

"We'll see."

◆

152

I was so excited that I didn't take the time to explain clearly to Ana what was going on.

She told me later that I came back from the phone in a state of high excitement and rushed out the door, muttering something about an illness in the family. If I had told Ana that I might be staying the night with Carmen she would have known where to find me when the shit hit the fan early next morning.

But it was left to the answering machine, once again, to be the bearer of bad news. How casually I turned it on when I came home the next morning from a blissful and unexpected night with Carmen, how dreamily I thought, It's Hamilton. . . .

In a voice of hysteria too frightened to be fake, he said that somebody had taken Delilah.

17

The morning had dawned hot and already I had lost the reckless desire of the night before. I stood there in the sunny, empty entryway by the answering machine, calling Ana's name and listening to the echo. I felt disoriented, as if I'd forgotten something essential or been gone for a very long time. Then I tried Hamilton's number at La Pedrera.

I let the phone ring a few minutes, imagining the sound beating like a heart in the fluid shapes of the Gaudí rooms.

The likeliest possibility was that Ben had decided she didn't want to wait to have a discussion with Hamilton about her parenting skills and had nipped over to the jazz club's kitchen and taken Delilah off once again. After all, she hadn't stolen her daughter yet; she'd probably been feeling left out. The reason that no one was answering at La Pedrera was that this time Delilah really was on her way out of the country, with her biological mother.

Of course Frankie could have been the one to steal Delilah again. Or maybe April and Hamilton had plotted something together. Maybe Hamilton's message on Ana's machine was just a bluff.

I tried to calm my mind. Whatever had happened I expected that I would know about it soon enough. There was nothing *I* could do anyway.

Accordingly I set myself to translation.

I had reached a chapter where past and present mingled,

where María had finally managed to locate her mother and to arrange a meeting with her.

In her old age Cristobel lived in the shabby mansion that Raoul had left her. Whatever he had carried in his black bag from village to village had made him wealthy but most of that wealth had been poured into right-wing political campaigns or leached away by his evil habits. With the passing of Raoul a whole generation of men also began to pass away, as if the strange potion, the tincture, the aphrodisiac with which he had infected them was losing its power. Almost to a one the elderly men of the country, statesmen and peasants alike, began to lose their manhood. As they moved into old age they grew breasts and their voices softened; their potency decreased rapidly. Some said that was the common fate of old men, to become old women, but in the eyes of the men themselves, their potency had been due to Raoul and contents of his black bag. Without that secret ingredient (something from the rainforest that now no longer existed?) they were doomed to ignominious femininity and then death.

I was making good progress and again entertaining fantasies of finishing the translation sooner than I had hoped, when around noon there was a determined ringing at the street door.

"Sí?" I called over the intercom.

"Cassandra, we know she's there, let us in!"

I buzzed them in without joy. At some point I really was going to have to put my foot down.

Frankie gave me a big hug. "Hi sweetie! I don't really suspect you, it's just that we have to make sure." She swept inside. "Well, isn't this *fascinating*. What is it, a museum?"

Ben was grim and stand-offish. "I'm sure she's here."

"Do you mean April or Delilah?"

"Delilah. Though I wouldn't put it past you to have April tucked away too."

"Ben, Ben, Ben," I sighed. "You keep suspecting me, but I'm telling you, I don't even particularly like kids."

"You don't have to like a kid to steal a kid," Ben said. She was back in her sleeveless tee-shirt and vest, with a red kerchief knotted around her neck. Her short blond hair had gel in it and stuck up like needles in a pincushion.

"To be honest, I thought you had Delilah," I said, leading the way to the living room. "I thought you wouldn't have wanted to wait until Hamilton brought her back, that you would have figured out she was at the jazz club."

"*I* figured it out," said Frankie. "But to tell you the truth, I decided that Hamilton had a point, and I've said this to Ben before. All this ruckus and fighting isn't good for Delilah. Ben and I have to make peace with each other, Ben has to make peace with me. So I persuaded Ben to stay home and spend the evening discussing things. Though I think she also wanted to be there in case the errant April returned."

Ben was ignoring us, swinging open closets, throwing herself on the floor to peek under couches, tossing aside drapes. If she was planning to really search this apartment she would be here forever. Even Ana's weekly housekeeper had areas she had long ago given up on.

My former employer lit a Camel and fluffed her curly wig.

"So what do you think happened to Delilah?" I asked Frankie.

"It's obvious. April alone or April with Hamilton has got her. I have no idea why, but I can tell you that when I get my hands on April, fur is going to fly."

Ben was in the bedrooms, pathetically calling, "Delilah? Delilah?"

"Why aren't you out looking for April then?"

"Because," Frankie struck a resigned attitude, "Ben refuses to believe that April is involved. We spent the whole morning at the consulate. You can imagine how wearing *that* was."

"I suppose Hamilton told you he dressed up as a woman to get Delilah out of the hotel yesterday morning?"

"Am I supposed to be shocked? Yes, he told us." Frankie paused and smiled. "Ben was shocked."

We followed the sound of Ben's footsteps through the apartment. She was in my room, under the eye of the figurehead, pawing through the pages of my translation. "You won't find any clues there, Bernadette; even Gloria de los Angeles couldn't have invented this plot."

Ben abruptly sat down on the edge of my bed and began to cry. "Oh, you can laugh," she said. "You and Frankie can make fun of me all you want. It's not *your* daughter."

"She is my daughter," said Frankie patiently. "And I told you she wouldn't be here with Cassandra."

"I don't know. I don't know anymore who's telling me the truth," Ben wailed.

Frankie sat down on the side of the bed and put an arm around Ben. I was struck by how practiced the gesture was, and how very tender.

"Look Ben," I said. "I'm sorry, but I think you have to face the fact that April probably has Delilah."

"You're just saying that," she sobbed into Frankie's sweater.

Frankie rolled her eyes at me.

"You also have to face the fact that April and Hamilton have something going on," I continued. "I don't know what but there's something."

"Hamilton says he hasn't seen April since the night I took Delilah," Frankie said.

"Lies, lies, lies," Ben broke down completely.

I hated to see a woman go pieces like that, especially one who looked like Arnold Schwarzenegger. Maybe it was time for me to offer to help again.

Besides, I still had April's book, *Stories the Feet Can Tell*. And I thought she might be wanting it.

It was about one o'clock, and the heat was building steadily. I left Ben and Frankie at La Pedrera with strict instructions to rest a little, and promised to call them if and when I came up with anything. Then I walked up to the Diagonal metro station and got on the green line going north.

If I started from the premise that April, who didn't like children much, had indeed taken Delilah last night, what would

158

she be doing with her today? She certainly wouldn't be inside playing cards. She might, in fact, be at the most obvious place of all.

When I found April she was sitting on the serpentine bench that wriggled around the elevated plaza at the Parc Güell. The bright fragments of mosaics glittered in the sun, a tile kaleidoscope of Mozarabic hexagons and romantic *fleurs de lis*, of diamond shapes and spirals, blues, yellows, oranges, discarded slivers from the tile factory pieced lovingly together again. Rumor had it that Gaudí had formed the curvatures of the benches by asking workmen to sit bare-assed on the wet cement, and something of that erotic request remained in the shape of the seats.

April was in pale yellow rayon, like a luscious jonquil. Her black hair coiled and curled over the ample shoulders of her tunic and her broad legs were softly encased down to her buttery socks and ever-present Birkenstock sandals. She looked like spring, except for the expression on her face, which was infinitely melancholy. She was reading deeply in a book entitled, in large letters, STRUGGLE FOR INTIMACY.

There was no sign of Delilah playing with the other children.

I slid into a warm mosaic seat next to her.

"April," I said. "Where have you been? All my life, I mean?"

"Oh Cassandra," she said, right on cue. "I was hoping to see you before my plane left."

"What do you mean, before your plane leaves?"

Her big black eyes were like blackberries, wet with a hint of purple.

"I have a flight to London tonight. Then I'll be flying back to San Francisco."

"I don't understand."

"No," she sighed. "Don't try to. Just accept."

"But Ben? And what about Delilah?"

"It wasn't working out. However much Ben wanted it to, we couldn't manage it. I need to be careful of women who want to sweep me off my feet. I'm an Adult Child," she confided.

I looked at her book. It was well-thumbed.

"You too?" she said.

"If you mean was my dad a sweet old Irish lush before his heart attack, yes; I am the grown-up child of this man. But I have good memories of him."

"You have intimacy problems, don't you Cassandra?"

This conversation wasn't going the way I wanted it to. "My life is a series of one-night stands and that's the way I like it," I said. "Now back to you, Miss Schauer. You're obviously not into casual sex, you're into commitment. So why are you really leaving your lover and her little girl?"

"Because Ben's true relationship is with Frankie, not me."

"Don't be daft. They're always fighting."

"They fight because they care a lot about each other. They always have." April stroked the cover of her book. "Frankie and Ben share a child. They both love her very much."

"They've got some funny ways of showing it."

"I did my best to find a place for myself in Ben's life. But I couldn't get along with Delilah. I don't like Delilah. And I was jealous of the relationship that Frankie and Ben had."

"Is that why you kidnapped Delilah? To punish them?"

"What do you mean?"

"Don't give me that, April. Delilah disappeared from the jazz club last night. Ben and Frankie didn't know she was there. You're the only one who could have known."

"But, but... No! I didn't know! I mean, I knew Hamilton knew that Frankie had taken her to that hotel and I guessed that he kidnapped her the next morning. But I didn't know... oh my god. Where could she be?"

"Let me see your plane ticket."

She pulled out her straw bag and fumbled through it. It was a single one-way fare to San Francisco by way of London.

And it occurred to me that April would have the same problem absconding with Delilah that Frankie would have had. Delilah was on Ben's passport, and April knew that.

"All right," I said. "Let's leave Delilah aside for the moment. Tell me about Hamilton."

160

Her dark eyes blinked. "What about him?"

"How did you meet him? The real story."

April paused. "He's my stepbrother."

"Your father was the one who married his mother? The mother in the Village?"

"Yes." April paused. "My mother and father met in Barcelona in the '30s. My mother was Czech, my father German. Jews. They thought Spain was safe, they bought an apartment—"

"In La Pedrera!"

April nodded. "But in 1942 they got out again. To New York. I was born a few years later, the only child. My mother died. My father married Nerissa Kincaid, Hamilton's mother. She's an alcoholic. It... it bound us together."

"He said you met in high school. Why didn't he just say that you were his stepsister? Why haven't you said anything before? Why doesn't Ben know?"

April stared at her book. "Hamilton and I both have a problem around telling people about certain things. We have Shame Issues."

"He told me about the struggle between his parents for custody. But he never mentioned you."

"I... we... what I'm saying is that we were close in adolescence, but we lost touch. He stayed in New York and went to school while I moved out to San Francisco and... came out. That's when we got in contact again. But he wanted to live abroad. So I sublet him the apartment."

"The apartment is actually yours then?"

"Yes."

"Oh April, April, you've made things so complicated," I said. "Yesterday you said you had something to tell me. Was this it? About Hamilton?"

She looked out at the sea. "Yes and no. Today I've realized that nothing is as important as we make it. You might understand, but you might not. Let's just cherish the time we've had together and thank the Goddess that we're still alive to struggle and change."

I took out *Stories the Feet Can Tell*. "Well, anyway, thanks for loaning this to me. I picked up a couple of useful tips."

I stood up, a little disappointed, but not really. In my profession you meet a lot of people. You can have them for a little while, but not forever.

"I'm sure we'll run into each other again, April," I said. "I don't mean in another life. But maybe at a march sometime."

"You have a good aura, Cassandra," April said, clutching her book. "Blessed be."

I always associate the end of the *siesta* in Spain with the sound of aluminum shop doors being rolled up again and fastened. The traffic picks up and people who have been sitting on benches along the streets or in cafés reading the newspapers reluctantly get up and go back to work.

I headed back to Ana's apartment, but she still wasn't there. On the answering machine were messages from Ben saying they hadn't found Delilah, from Frankie saying they hadn't found Delilah and from Hamilton saying he'd like to talk to me. I wondered when April was planning to tell them all she was leaving. To be on the safe side, I thought, at least one of us should be at the airport.

I was tired but reluctant to lie down after my nightmare the day before. I wandered into Ana's workroom to take another look at her progress with the houses, especially her amoeba shapes. I saw that she had lined one of them with velvet and experimented with joining them together. I bent down to investigate further and saw a bright blue sock and a white sneaker protruding from the fiberglass shape.

There was a small girl coiled in one of the ovular forms, like a mollusk in a shell. She had thin blond hair and glasses and was quite asleep.

18

I heard Ana come in the front door.

"You have some explaining to do," I told her when she appeared in the workroom.

"It was just for a little while," Ana said nervously.

"That's what they've all said."

"Well, you disappeared so quickly yesterday and I thought of the poor kid sitting in the kitchen playing cards all night... And I wanted very much to show her my houses and—"

"But why is she still here? Why didn't you contact her mothers?"

"She asked me not to."

"That's hard to believe."

Ana grew defensive. "She did. She said she didn't want to go back to everybody fighting over her. So I took her around Barcelona today, we went up to Poble Espanyol and took the funicular and then rowed a boat on the little lake in Ciutadella. You know, they hadn't really taken her anywhere, those mothers, they'd been too busy with their own affairs. And it was nice for me too, so nice being with a child."

I saw the white sneaker moving slightly.

"Are you awake, Delilah?"

"Uh-hmm," the mollusk answered.

I went over and looked at her. She wasn't a pretty child, but she had a sense of herself that I liked.

"Well, I don't need to tell you that everybody has been looking like crazy for you."

"Except April."

"I don't think April is going to be in the picture much anymore," I said. "If that makes you feel better. She's going back to America tonight by herself."

"That's good," Delilah said, and for the first time she looked happy. "So it will just be me and Ben and Frankie?"

"Yes, if they can work something out."

"I *hope* so," Delilah said, and began to crawl out of her shell. She stopped and looked at me. "You know the real reason that April didn't like me?"

"Well. . . "

"'Cause I figured out she was a boy."

"What!" both Ana and I said.

Delilah nodded sagely. "She was. Just like Frankie. A boy that turned into a girl."

"That's impossible, Delilah, you're confused. I mean, it's understandable that you would be confused, the way you've grown up. But I can assure you that April is not and never was a boy."

"Was too." Delilah made as if to curl back up in the shell.

"Okay, if you say so." Jeez, this kid needed counselling. And fast.

Delilah reluctantly climbed out.

"You ready to go back to Ben and Frankie?"

"Yeah. I guess." She turned to Ana. "Will you come with us?"

Ana was touched. You could tell she was having a struggle not to kidnap Delilah forever.

"I'll take you on the *moto*," she said.

"What about me?"

"It's just two blocks, Cassandra."

So I followed them on foot. Soon, soon, soon this would be all be over and I'd be on my way to London and then Bucharest. Tomorrow perhaps, after one last passionate night with Carmen. Any more and she'd be demanding that I move here. She was already demanding that I let my hair grow again.

The white waves of La Pedrera gushed around the corner and I saw Hamilton coming towards me from the Provença door.

"I met Ana and Delilah at the elevator," he said. "I'm so glad she's safe. It was a stupid thing for me to do, to take her from Frankie's hotel. It just made things more complicated."

There was no need to respond to that. I gestured to one of the white mosaic benches that seemed to emerge whole from the sidewalk of the Passeig de Gràcia. We sat.

"Hamilton," I said. "Why didn't you tell me that April was your stepsister?"

He started. "You've seen April?"

"At the Parc Güell. She told me the whole story of your childhood. She's on her way back to San Francisco tonight. She said she realized it would never work with Ben."

He was silent for an instant. "She told you the whole story?"

"Well, I think so. About her parents and your mother and the drinking and everything."

"Not the whole story then."

"What's the mystery here? Lots of people come from broken homes, lots of people come out, what's the big deal?"

Hamilton stared across the street at the rippling bulk of La Pedrera.

"April wasn't my stepsister."

"Oh god. Don't tell me she made that all up."

"Not exactly."

"What then?"

"She was my stepbrother."

"Stepbrother as in boy-brother?"

"Albert."

I leaped up and then sat back down again. "So Delilah was right."

Hamilton just nodded.

"Jesus Christ Almighty," I swore. "Does Ben know? No, of course Ben doesn't have a clue. Frankie must not either. Je-sus Christ."

"I'm not sure, but my guess is that when April got involved with Ben she didn't know about Frankie. Ben wasn't so eager for anyone to find out that she'd been married to a male-female transsexual. April may have thought that Delilah had a father she visited every weekend. But at some point she realized that Ben had huge problems with Frankie's transsexuality. Would April tell her if she thought that? Would you?"

"Probably not," I admitted.

"And the longer their relationship went on the more impossible it probably felt to discuss it. And then there was Delilah. Maybe Delilah said something to her. Maybe that's why she didn't like Delilah. I'm almost certain that's why she left San Francisco for Barcelona."

The hot spring afternoon was turning now to evening as Hamilton and I sat on the white bench looking at La Pedrera. A tinge of pink and peach from the sunset colored its porous surface, and it pulsed with undulant vitality, an expanding space rather than a static geometric configuration. It was wonderful—even so, if I'd only seen the outside I wouldn't have known that the real beauty of the building lay in the finely finished interior details, in its swirls of plaster and curves of dark woods, in the shapes of its rooms and the coils of its stairways.

"You know what Gaudí wrote about La Pedrera?" Hamilton said. "I've always liked this. He said '. . . the corners will disappear and the material will abundantly manifest itself in its astral rotundities; the sun will penetrate on all four sides and it will be the image of paradise. . . and my palace will be more luminous than light!'"

"That man was ahead of his time," I said. "Far *far* ahead. . . shall we go in?"

"No point saying anything about April to Ben now, is there?" Hamilton asked.

I shook my head, and then, companionably, we sighed and got up.

Frankie and Ben were sitting on the sofa with Delilah between them like a little prisoner of war. Ana was in tears, trying to explain her rationale for the kidnapping. Her usually competent English had deteriorated.

"I want. I only want make your girl happy. She so unhappy."

"Cassandra!" Frankie said as Hamilton and I entered. "This is the final straw."

"Oh, give it a rest, Frankie," I said cheerfully. "You got her back, didn't you? You got what you came for, didn't you?"

"But I've been *employing* you, Cassandra."

"Not recently."

"That's just like you, Frankie," Ben said. "You lie all the time."

"Oh you think you've been Miss Honest, Bernadette. You think you've been behaving with great honorability."

"Stop it!" shouted Delilah, jumping up from the sofa and running over to Ana. "I hate you both! I hate you talking like that! I'm sick of it!"

Ben and Frankie stared at her.

"But Delilah," said Ben after a moment, in a tone of adult reasonableness. "It's only that we love you."

"You should love each other!" the little girl screamed. "That would be better!"

Ben's face fell. "But we do love each other, honey."

Frankie sighed. "We do, Delilah. We just have a funny way of showing it."

She took Ben's hand. "Ben and I go back a long ways, Delilah. A lot of things have happened since we met, including you, a lot of changes. Some changes aren't easy to accept."

Delilah clung obstinately to Ana.

"We don't want you to be unhappy," Ben said, tears in her eyes.

"We want to be good parents to you," Frankie said.

Ana bent down and whispered something to Delilah, and slowly a smile appeared on the little girl's face.

"Okay," she announced. "But I want to go back home. And I want both of you to be nice to each other. Please."

Hamilton was coming undone beside me and suddenly left the room.

Frankie nodded. Ben nodded.

"Do you promise?" Delilah asked.

"Well, I've really been needing to get back to the gym," said Ben. "I'm completely out of shape."

"I promise," said Frankie, nudging her.

"I promise," said Ben.

Later I asked Ana what she'd whispered to Delilah.

"I told her I would give her one of my new houses to take with her. So she would always have a home."

19

I was back at the little square outside the church of Santa María del Pi, where Frankie and I had met that morning only a little more than a week ago. It was now the morning after Delilah had been found for good, and I was about to meet Ana and Carmen for a farewell coffee before my plane left for London.

I'd been doing some translation, because in spite of myself I'd gotten interested in the story of María and Cristobel and had made a pact with myself that I wouldn't skip to the end of the book to find out what happened. In my notebook, safely inside my leather briefcase beside me, I had almost fifty new pages translated, only twenty-five more to go. I would finish them in London, prepare a second draft and be well on my way to Bucharest by the beginning of June.

At long last the mystery of Raoul's black bag was solved! It contained nothing more, nothing less than. . . .

"Excuse me, is anyone sitting here?" a heavy German-accented English interrupted me. Its owner pointed to the table next to me, on the chair of which I'd settled my briefcase.

"Yes, all the tables immediately around me are occupied or will be shortly," I said in Spanish.

He sat down anyway, a young man with dark glasses and a ponytail.

"I'm here for a conference," he informed me.

"That's nice," I said, and returned to my pages.

He pointed to his flight bag, which he had set on the chair

on top of my briefcase. EUROPEAN SOCIETY FOR ORGAN TRANSPLANTATION.

Obviously he expected me to gasp, "Gosh, you must be a famous organ transplantor!" or "What *is* the European Society for Organ Transplantation? It sounds fascinating."

Well, sod him. Even if I were interested, I had work to do.

"I've seen you before," he announced, in another bid for conversation.

"I think that's very unlikely," I said haughtily. "I've just emerged from a remote location in northern Borneo where I was immersed in native culture for about twenty years. You're practically the first white man I've seen. I can't say your lot improved much while I was away, either."

"No, I am sure of it," he announced. "I have followed you twice. The first time I was quite lost. I had been looking at the cathedral but then I became disoriented. I wandered the streets. Then I saw you. I called after you to ask you directions but you started running. I realized you were afraid, so I ran after you to tell you I would not harm you. But you did not stop. Then, a few days later I saw you again late at night. Again, you did not stop."

"I had an urgent appointment. Besides, how did you know it was me?"

"Your jacket!" he said. "What a coincidence we meet now. My name is Wolfgang Schlagwurst. Herr Doktor Schlagwurst."

"Nice to meet you, Wolfgang. Now if you'll excuse me, I have a deadline to meet."

I turned my head away and tried to concentrate:

According to Cristobel the black bag, the ever-present mystery of her marriage, the curse of her wandering life on the river with Raoul, the mysterious piece of luggage that Raoul guarded with his life and that she believed if only she could open it would be her key to freedom and a new life, contained nothing more and nothing less than. . . .

"Cassandra, stop working!" Carmen bounced petulantly into a seat across from me. She withered Herr Doktor Schlagwurst's interest with a snap of her manicured fingers, which incidentally brought the waiter.

She ordered a *café solo* and took my hand in hers. "I'm very very angry with you, *querida*. You come to Barcelona by surprise and you leave by surprise."

I squeezed her fingers and said, "That's what life in the translation business is all about, Carmen. Speed, violence, sex, mystery. Translators come and they go, you can't count on them. You should never count on a translator. Or an organ transplantor for that matter."

"Cassandra, don't joke. You've broken my heart."

"It's better to leave when we're feeling good about each other," I said. "Besides, I'll be back."

"You said that last time."

"Well, I came back, didn't I?"

"But when?"

To my relief I saw Ana approaching across the square. Hamilton was with her. Why had she brought him?

"Ach, you have more company," said Herr Doktor Schlagwurst. "Then I will be going. So nice to have met you, *Fraülein*. And I apologize for having scared you."

I gave him a sudden smile. "In Northern Borneo," I said in Spanish, "somebody like you would be a nice snack."

He bowed politely and removed himself and his bag.

Ana and Hamilton sat down.

"I'm so sorry you're going, Cassandra," said Ana. "I feel as if I've hardly seen you."

If I allowed myself to really feel partings and farewells, I'd never have seen the countries and known the people I have. I closed my heart's door gently on sentiment and laughed, "You'll see me again. Probably when you least expect it."

"So is everything solved among your friends?" asked Carmen.

"Yes. Frankie and Ben worked out a new custody arrangement and have agreed to go into counselling. They're leaving tomorrow for home. And April left last night on a flight to London and then San Francisco." I didn't mention that I had gone to the airport to say good-bye to her. I wanted her to know that I wished her well, and that I thought Reflexology was probably the greatest new substitute for substance abuse ever invented.

"Delilah wrote me a note," Ana said, and pulled it out. "I think she dictated it to Frankie."

Dear Ana,
I think you are nice, you build neat houses, the one with the different parts is the best. Thank you for giving it to me, I know I will sleep really good every night. Thank you and good-bye, Delilah

Ana smiled at Hamilton and to my surprise took his hand.

"We have something to announce," she said. "Hamilton and I have been discussing having a child. He wants a family too."

Hamilton blushed. "It's a little unconventional, but I think it may work."

After all we'd been through it was astounding that anyone could use the word *unconventional.*

"Congratulations," I toasted them with orange juice. "Just remember: get everything in writing."

Ana laughed. "Oh, that reminds me. Here's something that will amuse you, Cassandra. After your adventures with pickpockets this trip." She took out a newspaper clipping from her pocket. It was from *La Vanguardia.*

A ring of thieves has come up with a new way to make off with the purses and bags of Barcelona's unwary citizens and tourists. Using flight bags from a conference that was held a week ago in Barcelona at Montjuïc, one or two skilled German thieves have taken upwards of fifty items. Yes, there really was a conference of the European Society for Organ Transplantation, but if you see these words imprinted on a flight bag anywhere near you—watch out!

Carmen said, "Cassandra, where's your briefcase?"
I looked at the seat next to me.
Cristobel and her long-lost daughter María had vanished.

♦

About the Author

Barbara Wilson is the author of three mysteries featuring Pam Nilsen, two novels and a collection of short stories. She has translated several works from Norwegian and received the Van de Bovenkamp-Armand G. Erpf award from the Columbia Translation Center for her work on Norwegian author Cora Sandel. She is a co-founder of Seal Press and, more recently, the non-profit publishing house, Women in Translation. She lives on Lake Union in Seattle.